FESTIVAL TURMOIL

SWEETFERN HARBOR MYSTERY #7

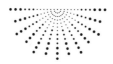

WENDY MEADOWS

MAJESTIC OWL
PUBLISHING LLC

CHAPTER ONE

SETTLING IN

$\mathcal{T}$he snow had fallen continuously in the week since Brenda and Mac had returned home from their honeymoon in Italy. Brenda took a deep breath and stood mesmerized by the sparkling winter wonderland surrounding the Sheffield Bed and Breakfast. There was nothing in her world to mar her happiness. The day she met Detective Mac Rivers, something stirred within her she had never experienced, and now after the marriage and the honeymoon, they were home again in her—now their—bed and breakfast. Mac returned to work that morning and Brenda Sheffield Rivers felt all was right with her world.

"You must land from your honeymoon, Brenda," Allie said. "It's back to business."

Brenda smiled at the teasing her young reservationist threw her way. Allie Williams was her youngest employee. She was adept in her responsibilities at the bed and breakfast and Brenda hoped she would remain in her job while attending the local college when the time came.

"I'm back," Brenda said, "but memories won't hurt anyone." She glanced at the computer. "Who do we have arriving today?"

"A couple is coming from upstate New York. They are Rachel and Thomas Wellington and should arrive early this afternoon. Then we have a man named Philip Turner from Canada." Allie named other guests who had either arrived or were due any minute.

"I know you need to practice your ice skating skills," Brenda told her. "Let me know when you'll need time off for that. We all want you to win during the Winter Festival later this week."

Allie laughed. "I want to win, too, but I've made arrangements to practice at the indoor rink in the evenings when I'm finished here. I hope the lake at the park is frozen solid enough to have the competition outside, though."

Brenda looked at the guest roster again. "It looks like we have one unreserved room. With the festival, I'm sure we'll have someone dropping in at the last minute for a spot here."

Allie agreed. It was rare that they had empty rooms, especially during special events in Sweetfern Harbor. She and Brenda commented on the heavy snowfall. They knew the snow alone would bring winter die-hards not only to their small town, but also to the popular Winter Festival.

At that moment the door opened, and Rachel and Thomas Wellington were welcomed in. They appeared to be in their early fifties. Rachel was petite in stature and remained somewhat quiet and reserved while Thomas signed in. He told Allie they came early to enjoy the village and shops before the festivities got underway. Brenda rang for Michael, who came to the foyer. He retrieved the bags and led the way for the Wellingtons to their room.

"I'm going to meet with the chef for a few minutes," Brenda told Allie. A brush of cold air swept the foyer at that moment. Brenda noted her reservationist's expression as she focused on the tall, good-looking man who walked toward them. His strides were determined and yet casual.

"Hello, I'm Philip Turner," the man said. He paused, his attention resting on Allie. "What is a beautiful girl like you doing behind a desk?"

Allie's face tinted a faint pink and she smiled up at him. His deep blue eyes riveted her attention. Thick hair the color of the sandy beach on the other side of the seawall

3

enhanced his looks. Allie saw the equipment bag by his side. "Do you have a hobby, Mr. Turner?"

"I'm a professional photographer," Philip stated. "I hope to get some good photos around town. I may start with you." He reached into his bag with a warm smile and retrieved an expensive camera.

Allie protested. "I know the Sheffield Bed and Breakfast is a nice backdrop, but perhaps you can wait to take my picture until I'm on the rink winning the upcoming ice skating competition?"

His eyes lit up with interest. "I will agree to wait to photograph you on one condition...you tell me everything you know about the activities planned for the festival," he said in a serious yet charming tone, and settled in to listen to Allie at length.

Brenda left them and headed for the kitchen. When she returned to the foyer, Philip had left for his room. Allie seemed to be in a good mood after her conversation with the photographer, but something was bothering her. She wanted to speak to Brenda.

"I know the empty room is the one that the famous actress Ellen Teague was murdered in, and I have a hard time assigning anyone to that room. Can't we just leave it empty?"

Brenda was surprised that Allie was still squeamish about that room. The incident had occurred only six months ago, but it felt like longer; and besides, the room had been occupied many times since with no complaints. Then she recalled the dead body disguised as a fake mummy someone left there during the Halloween tours, but somehow in Brenda's mind, that didn't count. She looked at her young receptionist.

"There is nothing to fear in that room," she told Allie. "Every time we have a full house it means you're even more secure with your job. Booking every room does pay our salaries."

Allie returned a half-smile. "I know I have to forget all of what happened that awful summer. I never tell anyone what happened in there and you are right. No one has experienced anything bad there since that time."

In the middle of the exchange, an older couple entered the bed and breakfast. Brenda felt sure they were the answer to filling the last empty room.

"My name is Richard Martin and this is my wife, Marilyn," said the tall, lanky man. He appeared to be in his sixties or so, and his shoulders stooped. His almost white hair and Romanesque features created a distinguished demeanor. His wife stepped forward and smiled. Richard continued. "I know we don't have a reservation, but we hoped you had an opening. We plan to stay in the area through the Winter Festival. Your bed and breakfast is gorgeous and inviting."

Marilyn stepped closer. "This Queen Anne structure is magnificent. What is the history of the house?"

"My uncle, Randolph Sheffield, was the owner until his death, when it became mine," Brenda said. "He prided himself on how well he kept it up. He was in the theater for many years and well-connected in the community, so many notable people have stayed here as well. He bought it because of its location along the Atlantic. It is beautiful, as you say."

A few seconds of silence passed while the couple's eyes rested on the architecture of the entrance and ornately carved staircase. Allie knew there was no option but to put them in Ellen's room. She halted her thoughts. Brenda never wanted the place referred to as Ellen's room. Instead, she cleared her mind and helped the guests register in the last open room. Once again, Michael was summoned. He retrieved the bags and escorted the couple upstairs. Marilyn stood a few inches shorter than her husband, but her head was erect and her shoulders back. Watching them ascend the stairs, Brenda would never have guessed she was any older than early forties, but her graying hair and faint wrinkles told otherwise when face to face.

Once everyone was settled in, Brenda went upstairs to the apartment she now shared with Mac. She called the detective to see how his first day back at work was going. She missed him already.

"It's good to hear your sweet voice, Brenda. It's hectic around here. Seems there have been several cases of burglaries around town while we were gone. Bryce told me they are on it but no viable leads yet."

"I'm sure Bryce has been doing everything he can. I hope you catch the culprit or culprits soon. That's not a good picture to show tourists who will be coming in for the Winter Festival."

"You're right about that. I want to solve it as soon as possible. Besides, we have to get started on plans for our new house."

Mac knew she smiled when she answered. "Yes, we have to start plans if we want to turn that summer house at the edge of the backyard into something livable." They returned to the subject of Bryce. Detective Bryce Jones was a young detective on the force. He was also engaged to Mac's daughter, Jenny Rivers. Both admired how Bryce had finally managed to gain some maturity since moving back to Sweetfern Harbor from New York City, and he had turned out to be very good at his job. Brenda felt that between Jenny and her father's influence, Bryce had come a long way.

"Be careful at Sheffield Bed and Breakfast, Brenda," Mac said. "Whoever the thief is seems to be hitting small businesses. I know you secure things well, but be on the alert anyway."

Brenda assured him she would do that. It felt good to have someone looking out for her and even better since that person was Detective Mac Rivers. They had improved the security of the bed and breakfast a little since her Uncle Randolph's day, but there was nothing quite like an officer of the law to make Brenda and her guests feel safe in their beds at night.

Out of curiosity, she made a mental note to ask Allie where the Martins were from. Knowing a little bit about the background of her guests was helpful when interacting with them during dinner or in the sitting room, where everyone congregated after meals and in the evenings. Dinner would be served at seven. She had an hour and a half until that time. She sat at her computer and typed up several ideas for new menus to present to her chef. She and Mac had found Italian food to be delicious on their honeymoon and she was anxious to start incorporating some of the regional dishes they had discovered into the menu.

The faint ring of the bell told her it was time to greet her guests at dinner. She glanced at her watch. Mac had not called back, but she decided his first day back on the job would likely prove to be a long one. She went downstairs and entered the dining room. Several guests were seated and waiting, amiably chatting about the festival and their time in the village. This group had no problem interacting with one another.

Brenda joined them and wished her housekeeper Phyllis was home to begin the new season with her. Phyllis Lindsey had married William Pendleton on Christmas Eve in a double wedding alongside Brenda and Mac. The Pendletons were due to arrive home from their island honeymoon the next day. Phyllis was not only Brenda's head housekeeper but had also become her best friend since Brenda arrived in Sweetfern Harbor.

Everyone had finished their salads and the servers were beginning to place the main entrées in front of guests when Thomas Wellington took his phone out of his pocket and suddenly excused himself.

"I really have to take this call," he explained. "It seems no matter how hard I try, I can't really leave my work at home."

His wife threw an anxious look in his direction. Brenda flashed him a reassuring smile and mentioned that the library down the hall was a good private place to take his phone call if he needed. He stepped into the hallway, out of everyone's earshot. When he returned, Brenda noticed the frown that crossed his forehead. But then Brenda was distracted when his wife Rachel's fork clattered loudly on her plate, and she twisted to look for her napkin. Without apologizing, she retrieved it from the floor. Thomas smiled at everyone and resumed eating, turning to ask his neighbor about their visit so far. Brenda dismissed the interruption as something Thomas Wellington would have to solve for himself.

"The winter landscape here is simply beautiful," Marilyn Martin said. "We rarely see a snowfall like this." When Philip asked her where they were from, Richard stepped in to answer.

"We are from the lower Midwest where we get ice more times than snow, but I agree with my wife. New England is a beautiful part of America." He turned to his wife. "We'll have to learn to ski while we're here."

She answered playfully. "You will have to do that without me. I'm not so sure I want to make such a fool of myself." They laughed together and soon stories around the table moved to skiing experiences. Brenda wondered where in the Midwest they were from. She originated from Michigan and that state got plenty of snow during the winter months.

After dinner, Brenda invited them into the sitting room for drinks. She heard Mac's footsteps coming from the back hallway until they reached the room where everyone was gathered. Mac's face was red from the cold and he went to the fireplace after Brenda introduced him to their guests. He rubbed his hands in front of the fire and accepted a cup of hot coffee from Allie. He sat next to Brenda on the sofa and chatted with the Martins. Brenda didn't miss how tired he looked. She stood up when he finished his coffee and together they told everyone goodnight.

Just as Mac stood back to allow Brenda to go ahead of him at the doorway, a sudden camera flash startled him.

"I hope you don't mind, I snapped a photo of you," Philip Turner said, lowering his camera. "I'm taking candid photos of everyone until the festival later this week."

"I have to say I would have preferred to be asked permission for you to do that, but I suppose no harm is done." Brenda knew Mac was distraught. He didn't like surprises like that.

Philip flashed a broad smile and said, "Good, I'm glad you're not upset with me."

In response, Mac's Robert Redford looks became steel. Without words, he and Brenda went up to their apartment. When they got inside, Mac relaxed.

"I'm sorry I treated your guest like that, but he should have asked before snapping a picture like that."

Brenda laughed. "He's your guest, too, or have you forgotten? Besides, he's young and needs to be taught some manners. You may have done him a favor."

"Come here, Brenda Rivers. I need to feel you close to me."

Brenda gladly accepted the invitation. "Tomorrow will be a better day for you, Mac. I know the first day back is the hardest."

Mac bent slightly and kissed his wife.

CHAPTER TWO

WANDERING GUEST

*B*renda's sleep was interrupted that night. She sat up in bed and tried to recall if she had a bad dream or perhaps been awakened by a sound. By now, she was fully awake and decided to close the bedroom door softly and escape into a book. Reading always calmed her and at this late hour, surely sleep would come soon. It took twenty minutes for this to prove correct. She stood to turn off the lamp and in the darkness that followed, she glanced through the window to the back lawn.

She did a double-take and squinted to focus better. A figure appeared to creep along at the edge of the tree line. From the slight stoop of the shoulders, she was sure she was looking at Richard Martin. The clock on the bookshelf read two o'clock. The snow was thick on the ground and the wind rustled the bare limbs of trees. The chill factor had to be unbearable out there, especially at this time of night.

"What in the world are you doing out like that in the middle of the night, Richard Martin?" She kept her voice low, not wanting to wake anyone.

She hoped this guest didn't have some sort of mental problem. It would take someone unstable to be outside at this hour in the deep snow. Brenda's next thought was to awaken Mac and tell him what she saw, but she recalled the weary look on his face and knew he needed his rest. She would tell him in the morning. He may have an explanation, though she wondered what it could possibly be.

As it turned out, Brenda missed Mac the next morning. His cell phone rang at five in the morning with the report of another burglary on the outskirts of town. This time, the victim was a young man who held classes in woodcarving. Several fine pieces of small furniture remained but three hand carving tools were missing.

When Brenda came downstairs for breakfast, she observed Thomas Wellington pacing across the front veranda with his cell phone to his ear. She greeted her guests in the dining room. Only Rachel Wellington seemed preoccupied. Brenda went up to her.

"Good morning, Mrs. Wellington. I hope you will get outside and explore Sweetfern Harbor as you said you planned to do, despite the snow." She smiled encouragingly at Rachel, thinking the couple could perhaps use some fresh air to escape whatever problems were going on back home. Rachel Wellington merely smiled and nodded distractedly, then turned to fetch another cup of tea.

Brenda worried a little for the couple. Sheffield Bed and Breakfast was intended to be a place for respite. Her mind swerved to Richard Martin. His wife Marilyn sipped coffee and conversed with a guest about her age. They were making plans to walk down to the shops when they finished breakfast.

"I think the town is so quaint and interesting," Marilyn said. She turned to Richard. "I don't suppose you want to come with us, Richard?" Richard picked up on the fact that his wife had asked merely out of courtesy and declined.

Richard's cheerful demeanor belied the fact he'd been roaming around outside in the very early morning hours. Brenda expected bags under his eyes from lack of sleep. Instead, he looked well-rested and she doubted whether she had really seen him.

Rachel Wellington picked at her omelet and even though she lifted the cup of hot tea, she failed to remember to take a sip. Brenda thought that Thomas Wellington had to have a strong constitution to spend that long outside talking on his phone in the cold.

Brenda finished her breakfast and asked the guests if anyone needed anything. Everyone answered in the negative and so she went to the office to catch up with Allie. It was time to make sure the night had gone well for guests and to see if anyone had any special requests.

"I told Mr. Wellington he could use the alcove off this hallway for his call," Allie explained. "He looked like he was freezing out on the veranda. It was my idea."

"I wondered how he could stand to be out there that long without a winter coat on." Brenda and Allie turned quickly toward the closed alcove door. Thomas Wellington's voice rose, though words spoken were not distinguishable to them.

"He doesn't sound pleased," Allie said.

"I just hope he and Rachel can get into town to get their minds off whatever the phone calls are about."

"Do you think we have an odd mixture of guests this time?" Allie asked.

Before Brenda could answer, a cold wind blew into the foyer from the small enclosure between the front door and the inside door. Smiles broke out on the women's faces. Hope Williams balanced a large box while edging inside. Brenda hurried to steady the door for her. Hope's face was pink from the cold.

"Why didn't you come through the kitchen door as usual?" Allie asked her mother. "Never mind. I don't care which door Sweet Treats Bakery goodies come through." She reached for a cinnamon roll dripping with white icing.

Hope laughed. "I came in this way because I knew I'd find the two of you in front. I know your habits," she said. Hope opened the lid and offered a freshly baked cherry muffin to Brenda. "This is a new recipe. Try it and tell me what you think."

Brenda took a bite and while savoring the tasty muffin, she nodded her head yes. Hope smiled gratefully and then her demeanor turned serious.

"I suppose you've heard about the break-in early this morning," she said. "I think whoever is committing these crimes doesn't do it to take anything of great value. It's as if he is taunting Sweetfern Harbor merchants."

Brenda hadn't thought about it that way, but Hope was right. So far, nothing of real consequence had been taken. The culprit or culprits were cunning and slick in their activities. The women chatted a little longer about the petty crime spree around town and then Hope said she must get back to Sweet Treats.

"Tourists are already arriving and I'll be kept busy." Allie offered to help her mother when she finished at the bed and breakfast. Hope told her to practice her ice skating routine instead. "How is the choreography coming along?"

Allie Williams was a talented young woman and figured everything out by herself. She didn't want to tell anyone details of the routine she had in store for the competition. Hope had long ago given up on trying to pry specifics from her.

"It's coming along fine. I just have a few things to smooth out, but I'll be ready." Allie smiled mysteriously but excitedly.

After Hope left, Brenda decided it was time to loosen the spirits of the Wellingtons. She looked for them and saw Rachel coming from the dining room.

"Any decision yet? Are you and Thomas going downtown today?" Brenda asked. "There are many specialty shops that I think you'll find interesting." She told Rachel about Morning Sun Coffee, Jenny's Blossoms, the shop that sold crafts created by area residents and the other places of interest. "There's also an interesting museum if you want to learn more about our town."

"I hope to get down there," Rachel said. Brenda didn't think she sounded convincing.

"I know you will enjoy the Winter Festival but do visit

the town. You won't be sorry." Brenda smiled but did not get one in return.

Rachel continued to be distracted. "I'm looking for Thomas." When Rachel turned from Brenda, the Martins came into the hallway. Richard spoke to his wife and told her to have a good time in town. Marilyn and her new-found friend Linda went upstairs to retrieve their coats and gloves. Brenda told them Michael would be happy to take them and anyone else downtown and pick them up later.

"We want to walk. The sun is out," Marilyn said, "and the wind has let up some. It will be good to get out into the fresh air."

Brenda wished them well and watched Richard. When his wife left, his face changed. Furrows formed across his forehead. He hesitated at the bottom of the stairs and seemed to be observing the landing at the top before he climbed the steps.

Brenda decided to quietly follow him from several steps behind. When Richard got to the top of the stairs he noticed her behind him. At first, his startled look surprised Brenda, until the smile spread across his face. The image of a chameleon ran through Brenda's mind.

"What is at the end of this hallway?" he asked.

"The guest rooms end three doors down from here. Then there are closets where housekeeping supplies and equipment are kept. Around the corner is our apartment. It's almost a separate wing."

"When was this place built?"

Brenda explained it was circa 1890. She told him how it had changed hands a few times until her uncle purchased it, and how it became hers. Richard Martin appeared genuinely interested in its history.

"Are you a history buff?"

He laughed and shrugged his shoulders. "I suppose an amateur one at best. I've found history in areas like this to be interesting."

"Then you will love exploring downtown. Every shop along the main thoroughfare is on the historic register."

He promised to do just that and turned toward his room. Brenda continued to her apartment. She wanted to ask him about his stroll around the premises in the very early morning hours, but decided to discuss it with Mac first. Once in her apartment, she began to doubt again that she had seen Richard Martin at all. But who else could it have been?

She did not hear the quiet pad of footsteps on the carpet of the second-floor hallway as Richard Martin crept out of his room and explored, once more alone.

Brenda set the water to heat in her teakettle, absorbed in her thoughts. She missed Phyllis and was disappointed that she and William had delayed their arrival home an extra two days. She couldn't blame them. Phyllis had waited almost fifty years to find the man of her dreams and Brenda understood how the couple wanted to spend as much time together as possible. When they returned, both would be involved in the Winter Festival. Sheffield Bed and Breakfast would keep Phyllis busy once again. Everyone in town would gather there after the final competitions for hot chocolate and an array of finger foods and treats to end the celebration.

Brenda had come to look forward to the seasonal events that occurred in Sweetfern Harbor. At first, she couldn't understand why the townspeople seemed to search for ever-constant ways to celebrate. It had all become second nature to her after her first year, and she looked forward to every one, and in particular to hosting the town that night.

At noon, Brenda searched for Allie. Sheffield Bed and Breakfast had grown quiet and she felt Allie could use a break. She wrapped up in layers and went downstairs. Allie was all too ready to grab her coat and walk with Brenda. They walked briskly toward town down the shoveled paths through the snowbanks on the sidewalks.

"I haven't seen Jenny more than once since Mac and I got back," Brenda said. "Let's stop at Blossoms first."

Jenny greeted them and hugged them both. "I hope I see more of you, Brenda, but I know you and my dad had a lot of catching up to do at work when you got back." She pulled back and the smile that went from the corners of her mouth widened. "I'm so happy you joined our family."

Jenny had missed her mother since the day the disease took her away from her and Mac. She was thrilled she had a mother again. Brenda proved to be a best friend, too.

"I'm happy about that as well, Jenny. I've always wanted a daughter and couldn't have found a better one."

Jenny showed them her new display in the window. It was a replica of the hill at the end of Sweetfern Harbor just before reaching the seawall. With a sparkling carpet of snow and tiny, glowing streetlights, the display was just as magical as the town itself on a snowy night. Brenda and Allie told her it was perfect.

Despite the perfect day and the light conversation, Brenda wanted to caution Jenny to pay attention to her customers, in the event someone came in to case the shop for burglary. She hesitated since she was sure Mac had done that more than once.

"I know what you are thinking, Brenda," Jenny said. "Bryce stops in here several times a day and my father has told me what to look for in case someone comes in who looks suspicious. Bryce has become a mother hen." Brenda could tell Jenny was happy her fiancé was solicitous.

"That's good. I knew I was right—both detectives are looking after you quite well."

Brenda and Jenny, with Allie's help, chose arrangements to be delivered to the bed and breakfast the morning of the last festival day. All agreed the flowers would be perfect and once everyone saw what Jenny had done with them, she was sure to have an even bigger increase in customers.

Next, they stopped at Morning Sun Coffee to warm up. Tucked into a booth with their coffee mugs warming their hands, Molly sat with them for a few minutes.

"Can you believe my mom and William have delayed coming home again?" she asked. Then she laughed. "I don't blame them. William has made my mother so happy, but I miss her."

"I miss her, too, but she should be back in a day or so. Sweetfern Harbor needs William here and I need Phyllis."

On the way home, Brenda thought again about the Martins and the Wellingtons. Sweetfern Harbor was as joyful as ever with the festival ahead, but maybe Allie was right. Some of her guests did seem to be unsettled for some reason. She resolved to find ways to help them relax and discussed the matter with Allie as they walked along.

CHAPTER THREE

STRANGERS IN TOWN

"Mac, I'm glad you're home in time for dinner tonight," Brenda said. "Before we go downstairs, I want to tell you about something I saw last night."

She told him in detail about the figure at the edge of the band of trees. At first, Mac chided her for not telling him sooner, but realized Brenda had some doubts about what she saw or didn't see.

"You don't make mistakes like that, Brenda. With all the petty crime going on around here, I'm on edge. If anything like that happens again, tell me right away. If I'm not here, call me, or if I'm asleep, wake me up."

Brenda apologized and realized how important it was.

She wished she had told Mac when it happened. His warm kiss soothed her.

"The reason I doubt myself is because Richard was very cheerful this morning and didn't look like he had lost any sleep at all."

"Any way that you look at it, it was strange that anyone was up at two in the morning trudging through snow. What was he doing out there? Did you see anyone else with him?"

Brenda shook her head. "To my knowledge he was alone, unless someone was hidden. The yard light didn't shine all the way to the tree line, so I suppose there could have been someone else out there."

While they discussed the subject, Mac's phone rang. The look of panic on his face alarmed Brenda.

"Where's Jenny?" he said to the caller.

When he ended the call, he grabbed his coat. "Is Jenny all right?" Brenda asked.

"She's fine but her shop was just broken into, and her window display was left destroyed. She and Bryce were at my house. I'll call Bryce and tell him to bring her here until we canvas the shop."

Brenda had never seen anger like the one that seethed in Mac's eyes. "I'm coming in my car," she said. "I'll pick up Jenny and bring her here." When Brenda arrived at Mac's former house, she went inside to find a female police officer handing Jenny a hot beverage. Brenda identified herself to the officer while Jenny clutched her arm and set the drink down. Brenda swung her into a tight hug.

"Your dad wants you to come home with me and stay at the bed and breakfast."

"Bryce told me he would stay here with me when he gets back in."

"They may both be on this all night long. Come with me so your dad won't have to worry about you, Jenny."

The officer agreed with Brenda, and all three gathered Jenny's belongings. She secured the house and the officer followed them until they were safely inside Sheffield Bed and Breakfast. That was when Jenny sank onto Brenda's sofa and shook like a leaf in a strong wind. Brenda pulled her close. They were in the apartment, away from prying eyes, and Jenny could finally let out the emotions she had been bottling up inside. The tears ran down her face.

"Everything will be all right, Jenny. You are safe here and you can be sure Bryce and your dad will get to the bottom of it all. He called in the state police for help. I expect there will be more law enforcement brought in as well."

Jenny's sobs subsided, and she began to relax. Brenda shifted her from the couch to an easy chair while she pulled the sofa into a bed. She made up the bed and told Jenny it was ready when she was. Finally, Jenny laughed.

"I never go to bed this early, but I'm glad it's ready when I am."

Brenda offered her something to eat. "There is plenty downstairs in the refrigerator and I have soup and crackers up here in our little kitchen."

Jenny declined. "Bryce and I had a wonderful dinner at the local Italian restaurant, so I've had all I need for now." She bent her head into her cupped hands. "I can't imagine who would destroy my window display like that. Most importantly, why would anyone just break in to destroy things? I have some valuable vases and urns in there and they were left intact. Nothing significant was taken as far as I know. I know they haven't done a complete investigation yet, but I doubt anything was stolen." Brenda shook her head. She had no answers. Jenny wanted to talk. "You know, Brenda, everyone who owns a business in Sweetfern Harbor is on edge and very nervous. So far the thefts have happened after hours...but we are all wondering how long it will be before the thieves get more brazen and possibly harm someone."

"This is why we have an excellent police force in Sweetfern Harbor. You know your dad is an expert in his job, and Bryce is too. There are several other officers we both know who will do everything in their power to solve the crimes."

"I hope you give your input, too, Brenda. You have insights sometimes that the law doesn't see right away."

Brenda beamed inside. It was true. She had found solutions to several crimes that occurred since her arrival in Sweetfern Harbor. "I'm paying attention to what is going on, Jenny. If I come up with anything I'll definitely let Mac know. Chief Ingram is sometimes reticent in his behavior but he is always on top of things, too."

Jenny smiled. "Bob is an excellent friend and as Chief of Police, he's the best thing that happened to Sweetfern Harbor."

"Then it's settled. We'll keep our eyes open and let them do their work."

The muscles in Jenny's body relaxed and she sank back into the overstuffed chair.

Thomas Wellington closed the door to the room he and his wife shared. She sat on the edge of the bed with a worried look on her face.

"Are things moving along better, Thomas?" she asked.

"There is nothing to worry about, Rachel. There have been a few hang-ups but things are smoothing out."

"I hoped to relax and see a little of the area around here. It would be a wonderful place to visit in the summertime. I hear they have annual boat races. Do you remember how we met on that sailboat your friend had in Florida?"

Thomas smiled. "I remember. That was a long time ago when I think about it. It was a more innocent time for both of us. I was no sailor, but you took to the water like a fish in the ocean. It would be nice to come back in better weather. I'm not a fan of winter, especially like this one."

Rachel thought about the years since that day when she met the handsome Thomas Wellington. It had been a rocky road for both of them. More than once she almost decided to leave him for someone more stable. There was something about Thomas that always drew her back to him. Now they were full partners in business.

Because of his business interests, he had convinced Rachel that it would be profitable to attend Sweetfern Harbor's Winter Festival. She hoped he planned his venture well and was successful.

Down the hall, Richard Martin knew an argument was brewing with his wife. Marilyn nagged him for not spending much time with her during this getaway. She knew Richard had little interest in shopping. He seemed to appreciate historical sight-seeing and architecture but even that interest appeared to remain on the surface as far as she could tell.

She had been married to him for six years and just when she thought she had him figured out, he turned out to be someone entirely different. She was his third wife and when they married, she felt sure she would be his one and only for the rest of their years. As the years passed, she felt he was not the man she thought she married, but she tended to shove those thoughts from her mind.

Richard could carry on a brilliant conversation about most things the guests discussed during meals and in the sitting room, and he was an avid reader. He could also read people very well. When he sensed someone had an interest in a specific subject, he read up on it and became knowledgeable enough to converse amicably about it.

"If you are truly interested in the 1800s, I would think you'd want to explore this town a little more. Linda and I met so many nice people today. One shopkeeper told us that when someone named William Pendleton returns home we should meet with him. William is a historian and knows the entire history of this area."

"Marilyn, I'm only interested so I can join in conversations in an intelligent way. Someone like me shouldn't come across as someone who has no knowledge in matters of history."

Marilyn stared at him, thinking his words didn't make complete sense. "Someone like you? What does that mean, exactly? It's funny, but I realize I don't know very much about your past, dear. Where were you born, for instance?"

"I was born in New Mexico, but I told you my father was in the service and we constantly moved around. There's nothing else of note to tell you." He paced a few steps and turned to her. "I need a good brisk walk in the cold air."

"It's time for bed. What in the world moves you to go out in the cold night? Let's go down to the sitting room and drink something hot in front of the fireplace instead."

Richard waved his hand impatiently. "I don't need a hot beverage. I need fresh air." He needed a stiff drink, too, but after years of resisting that old habit, he dismissed the thought.

He took his winter jacket off the coat tree in the corner of the room. Marilyn looked at him. Maybe her sister had been right in advising her not to marry him, stating there was something not right about the man.

Richard headed past the sitting room. Voices floated from the room as he went out the front door. He stood on the top step of the porch and breathed deeply. There was a lot to think about. He walked to the seawall and back several times and then decided his wife must be asleep by now. By the time Richard returned inside, the sitting room was empty. He glanced at his watch, which read eleven-thirty. He was finally relaxed enough to sleep well and soon his head hit the pillow in a deep sleep.

After an evening of conversation, Brenda had finally coaxed Jenny to go to bed. Despite her protests, the young woman had fallen asleep before Brenda could even finish putting away their tea mugs in the kitchen. She pulled the blankets up to cover Jenny and went into her bedroom to get ready for bed. Mac and Bryce were still out and she didn't expect to see either until morning. Brenda was glad that they could concentrate on the crimes knowing Jenny was safe with her. She was pleased to sleep after a day of tending to Jenny and fell quickly into dreamland when she laid down.

The next morning, Brenda awoke and realized Mac was not there. She felt his side of the bed. It was cool and the sheets were not even disturbed. She sat up and sorted her thoughts. She was sure she would have known if he had come in late. She was sensitive to movements and noises, even of the slightest nature. Brenda decided to shower and dress. To not disturb Jenny, she would have her first cup of coffee downstairs. When she came into her living room, she was surprised to see the couch had been made up and folded back into place. Jenny had left a note on the coffee table.

Brenda—I'm going to my shop. I feel much better today, much stronger. I need to meet with the officer at my shop to determine for certain if anything is missing. I promise I will be back around mid-morning, right after I pick up a change of clothing from home. -Jenny.

Brenda felt panic after reading the message. She wanted Jenny right there with her like she had promised Bryce and Mac. She wasn't sure whether to call Mac and alert him, or trust Jenny's instincts. However, Jenny was a grown woman after all, and a business owner with pressing matters to deal with. She decided Jenny would be fine for now.

Allie came in the door just as Brenda got to the bottom step. The young woman's face was flushed from the cold. She smiled brightly. Brenda groaned inwardly and for the hundredth time wondered how anyone could be so cheerful so early in the morning.

"I brought donuts from Sweet Treats to get you started this morning, Brenda." Allie set the box on the counter and unlocked the office door. "Today will be a great day since Phyllis and William are coming home."

That did perk Brenda up. She missed Phyllis. They always had early morning coffee together and talked about the day ahead. Together they could slowly wake up in peace.

"I will be so happy to see them safely back home," Brenda said. "Let me know the minute they get here. I'm going to the dining room to have a little breakfast if you need me."

Two guests were ahead of her at the buffet. They had been the first ones downstairs each of the three mornings since they booked into the bed and breakfast. The woman told Brenda their plans for the day. It seemed they were ready to do more exploring. After she finished her meal, Brenda went into the kitchen.

Chef Morgan was sipping coffee. "Have you seen Mac this morning?" Brenda asked her.

"The last time I saw him he was going up the back steps an hour or so before I left last night. He must have left pretty early this morning, if you haven't seen him."

Brenda looked at her chef and asked what time she saw him. Morgan said she had stayed later than usual to prepare some food for the crowd expected after the Winter Festival. A deep foreboding swept through Brenda. She had been up last night with Jenny, and Mac had not come into the apartment. She thought he must have come home to the bed and breakfast but then been called out again before he made it upstairs. Even that notion didn't sit well with her since she knew he would generally check on Jenny and her before leaving again.

Brenda went into the small alcove off the main hallway and closed the door. She called Mac. There was no answer except for his voicemail. She then dialed Bryce.

"Is Mac with you, Bryce?"

"No. I haven't seen Mac since last night, when he headed home. Didn't you see him this morning?"

"I didn't..." Brenda swallowed. She felt a cold feeling in the pit of her stomach.

Bryce picked up the panic in Brenda's voice and told her he would be right there. Bryce tried to calm down so he could think clearly by the time he got to the bed and breakfast.

"Brenda, keep calm. For Jenny's sake and for yours, no one should expect the worst before the facts are sorted out." Brenda thanked Bryce for the reassurance as they ended the call and she sat down to wait for him, tense and silently clutching her phone for reassurance.

CHAPTER FOUR

VICTIMS

By the time Bryce arrived at the bed and breakfast, Brenda had called Chief Ingram and apprised him of the situation. Bob Ingram had known Mac Rivers most of his life. It was highly unlike his detective to not check in with his boss or with his own wife. The fact that Mac's own daughter's shop had been broken into only increased the questions in his mind. The chief called the two officers at Blossoms and when told Mac had not been there, he became more worried. He radioed Bryce and told him he would meet him at the bed and breakfast in five minutes.

Brenda met Bryce in the foyer and they went upstairs to her apartment for privacy. "Where's Jenny?" Bryce asked, looking around.

Brenda showed him the note. Bryce's eyes darted around

the room again as if to make sure Jenny wasn't sitting there as he expected. He quickly called one of the officers at Blossoms and told him that when Jenny arrived to tell her to stay there until he came for her. The officer told him he had been there for several hours and hadn't seen her.

"Perhaps she went somewhere else," Bryce mused.

"The note did say she needed a change of clothing. Maybe she went home first? Maybe she's still there..." Brenda realized both her husband and stepdaughter were possibly missing. There was no logical reasoning to any of it at the moment. "Send someone to Jenny's house." Bryce nodded and radioed to the dispatch officer at the station, and a police officer was sent to the Rivers home.

Brenda paced in a tight circle but knew answers would not come immediately. "In the meantime, let's look for any more signs of Mac. My chef Morgan said that Mac came in and went up the back stairs around eight last night. Jenny and I didn't see him at all, which means he may never have made it all the way up to the apartment."

At that moment, Chief Bob Ingram came into the room. Brenda told him about Jenny and Mac. The chief told Bryce to search the back stairwell and anywhere in that area. "Be careful and don't disturb anything we might need as evidence later." Then he saw how white Brenda's face had turned. "Don't worry, Brenda, he may have gotten a call and gone back out before he had time to make it all the way up. Your chef could have had her back turned and not noticed he went back out."

Brenda nodded. She followed Bryce and the chief down the back hallway to the stairs. Bryce held up his hand for them to stop and be silent. Soft moaning came from somewhere nearby. The chief turned back to Brenda and told her to wait where she was. Brenda's stomach was in knots and she stood frozen in the hallway, listening.

The officers proceeded down the hallway, which appeared empty, until another moaning sound filtered out from behind a closet door. Bryce yanked it open to find Detective Mac Rivers crumpled on the floor. The fresh, livid welt on the side of his head caused Bryce to immediately dial for emergency services. He told the dispatcher to come to the back of Sheffield Bed and Breakfast. He then turned to Chief Ingram.

"I have to go find Jenny. She may be in danger."

Brenda shoved the officers aside and gasped when she saw Mac in a heap on the floor of the supply closet. She quickly knelt down beside him and called his name several times. His eyes fluttered and he attempted a reassuring smile. As soon as the brief exchange ended, his eyes closed again and he fell into unconsciousness.

"Mac, Mac," Brenda called to him. "Please wake up, Mac." Chief Ingram gently touched her shoulder. Her tear-filled eyes threatened to overflow.

"Brenda, leave him where he is until the paramedics get here. He will be fine once he wakes up completely. That knot on his head will be painful and he'll have to deal with that. He will be fine," the chief repeated. He hoped he was telling the truth. Sirens could be heard as the ambulance crew arrived and trooped in through the rear entrance.

Both stood up and let the medics take over. Brenda sprinted back to the apartment to grab her coat and then followed the paramedics down the back stairs to the ambulance. Chief Ingram called another officer to escort the ambulance and told him to take Brenda with him to the hospital.

"Brenda, I'll be at the hospital as soon as we're finished here. We have a crime scene to process and when one of my officers has been assaulted, I will leave no stone unturned. I will personally oversee the crime scene processing," Bob Ingram told Brenda, his mouth set in a firm line.

Brenda nodded, still a little numb with shock. She realized that most guests had no idea that anything was amiss. Some had already left for the day or were eating a late breakfast. Allie Williams ventured upstairs just then and the chief told her to keep mum until further notice. Her stricken eyes met Brenda's and she hugged her boss tightly before letting her go. No words were exchanged. There were no appropriate ones that could be voiced.

In the squad car, Officer Patrick Simpson attempted a conversation that hopefully would distract his boss's wife. He pointed out the beauty of the snow and when they passed the park, he commented on how beautiful the winter decorations looked. Brenda returned a faint smile and found she wanted to face what was going on rather than discuss meaningless topics.

"I hope his condition isn't too bad," she said. She had to start somewhere, she thought.

"I'm sure he will be fine. I saw his eyes flutter open and shut. He'll come to completely and be back to his old self before you know it."

"That's what I'm hoping. Is there any word on where his daughter is yet?" Brenda almost chided herself for forgetting that officers had been sent to look for Jenny at her house.

"I know everyone is looking for her. I'm sure she is fine, too. I understand she was on her way to her shop. It's a shame when I think about what's going on in this peaceful little town. Everyone is looking forward to the Winter Festival but they're worried, too. Something's going on, but don't you worry, I'm sure we will solve it soon."

Brenda was relieved when they arrived at the hospital. All protocol was set aside when they learned an officer of the law had been assaulted, and Mac was taken to a private room right away. When Brenda came to the doorway, several doctors were examining Mac. She knew he was going to be all right when he protested having to be in bed.

"I'm fine. Just let me out of here so I can get back to work."

Dr. Young's voice was more reassuring to Brenda than to Mac. "You'll be back at work once we know you aren't going to collapse on us again."

Chief Ingram came up behind her. "That sounds like he's going to be fine for sure. You can come in with me, Brenda, while I ask Mac questions. I hope he knows who did this to him. I believe whoever attacked Mac has a lot to do with the petty crime wave around town."

As it turned out, no doctor was going to allow Detective Mac Rivers to leave the hospital before the next day, and then only after a thorough examination. His concussion was serious and they were concerned that a blood clot could have caused him to pass out, so they were planning to scan him thoroughly.

Brenda held Mac's hand while the chief questioned him about his attacker. Mac forced himself to numb the feelings of pain and finally shook his head slightly.

"I didn't see who it was. I just know that one blow like that had to come from someone strong and either my height or perhaps taller."

"Did you pick up any notable odors, like cigarette smells, or perhaps an after-shave, anything like that at all?"

"I remember coming up the steps and I was almost to the small landing where the stairs turn before continuing up. Just as I stepped around the corner to the next set of steps, I felt the blow to my head. Whoever it was either followed me up quietly or came from that narrow closet at the landing from behind me. I take it he dragged me on up and threw me in that closet." Brenda squeezed his hand tighter. "Don't worry about me, Brenda. I'll be fine. Obviously, whoever it was meant to scare me. If he'd wanted to kill me, he had the privacy and time to do so." Brenda shuddered.

The chief had already gotten the report from one of his officers who interrogated Chef Morgan. She had not seen anyone come in the back entrance except for Mac, who she thought had gone upstairs. She had seen no one come back down and leave by the back door either. She explained she had been in the dining room part of the time after she saw Mac, who had waved to her before going in. Back in the kitchen, she worked at the table near the pantry with her back to the entry. She heard nothing at all.

Brenda spent the entire day with Mac while he endured a battery of tests and bloodwork. He finally insisted she leave long enough to get something to eat in the cafeteria. She realized then that she had not seen Bryce since he left to help look for Jenny. Brenda agreed to get something to eat, not wanting to tell Mac about Jenny just yet.

She told the officer stationed at the door of Mac's room that she was leaving for a few minutes. At the elevator, Bryce stepped off just as she was ready to step on. His face was drained and his eyes held fear and worry.

"What's wrong, Bryce?"

"We can't find Jenny anywhere. Is Chief Ingram still here?"

"He left for a half hour and will be back. What did you find out, Bryce? You look white as a ghost."

He held out a clear plastic evidence bag with a note inside. "An officer found this in the closet where Mac was left." He held it while Brenda read it. "This is a warning," she read out loud, "to remind you that you caused hell to rain on me when you made sure I went to prison." Brenda didn't speak. Bryce put his arm around her shoulder.

"I know Mac wants out of here, but the doctors say no to that. You have to convince him we're doing everything we can," Bryce said. "We've assigned two officers who have worked on cases with Mac to investigate who may be out to get him. It has to be someone recently freed." He wrung his hands. "I have to find Jenny."

Brenda's heart beat faster. She could only nod her head. All appetite left her and she went back to the room with Bryce, who thought he should make an appearance before returning to look for his fiancé again. Just then, Chief Ingram came down the hall and Bryce turned to give him the news and hand over the note after he reinserted it into the evidence bag. Together they paused before going into the room and mutually agreed not to tell Mac they still hadn't found his daughter. Brenda knew he would soon wonder why Jenny hadn't come to see him. Brenda had attempted calls to her with no results.

Brenda left Mac's room when more officers arrived. She said she wanted to go home and get her own car plus extra clothes so she could spend the night at the hospital with Mac. Everyone knew her well enough to not protest her plans. Officer Simpson again accompanied her home. As they drove away, Brenda glanced at her watch. It was four in the afternoon and no one had located Jenny Rivers yet. She knew before night fell she would have to tell her husband his daughter was missing.

Brenda barely heard the attempts at conversation from Officer Simpson as he drove through the streets of Sweetfern Harbor. Something nagged at her about her guests. If the assailant had gotten inside the bed and breakfast, then it was very likely a guest or staff member who did this to Mac. She dismissed her staff. Everyone had been checked thoroughly before she hired them. The references included criminal background checks. None had any encounters with the law except traffic tickets or a similar minor infraction. Besides, she could not think of anyone on her staff who would be tall or powerful enough to manage such a blow to Mac's skull.

She asked Patrick to let her out at the rear entrance of the bed and breakfast and thanked him. "We'll find whoever is responsible, Brenda," he said.

She nodded. "I know you will, but the sooner the better. We must find Jenny above all." His heart was heavy when she spoke the words. Officer Simpson nodded, well aware of the priority.

Brenda entered the back hallway. As she passed the entrance to the back stairwell, she averted her eyes rather than glimpse the crime scene tape. She opted to continue down the hall and use the front stairs. The reminder of what had happened to Mac was something she wasn't ready to face yet. From the sitting room, she heard Rachel Wellington's voice. From the deeper-toned response, she knew Thomas was with her. She decided it was most important to continue business as usual for her guests, so she ducked her head in and greeted them. Both looked surprised to see her but quickly regained their composure. In answer to her question, they told her they didn't need anything. Brenda turned and left them.

At the bottom of the stairs, she heard a scream coming from the room she'd just left. When she got to the doorway, her heart hammering in her chest, Thomas was peering through the window. Rachel's ashen face was a mask of fear.

"What happened?" Brenda asked. Rachel pointed to the window. Brenda followed her line of sight. Thomas paced and then stared into the yard. Rachel found her voice.

"There was a creature with dark eyes staring at us. He pressed his face right up against the window and made threatening signs toward us."

In the winter, this time of early evening was already dark. However, Brenda took note that it was possible to see dark eyes if pressed on the glass, due to the light inside. The windows were such that one could look out and have a clear view, but anyone outside was prevented from peering inside the room unless they were right up next to the glass.

Rachel twisted her fingers until they resembled knots. Thomas glanced again through the window.

"Whoever it was is long gone now," he said. This did not reassure his wife. "There's nothing to worry about. Someone just tried to get us upset by playing a prank on us. Probably a teenager."

Rachel sat down and then jumped back up. "I'm not so sure, Thomas. Those eyes were menacing. Who was it?" She sat back down and clasped her hands tightly.

"Don't worry about it. I'll take care of things," Brenda said. "We'll get to the bottom of it and whoever it was won't do it again." She wished Mac was here. Instead, she went into the hallway away from her guests and called Bryce. Wearily, she explained what had happened and requested assistance.

Detective Bryce Jones arrived in a short time with several state police. They combed the premises and the nearby streets and yards and questioned the Wellingtons several times.

"There is no one on your premises, Brenda, or in the neighborhood." Bryce's forlorn look told her he hoped they would find whoever it was. He didn't have to say out loud what they were both hoping—that this could be a clue leading to the person who attacked Mac.

"It's all right, Bryce. I need to get back to the hospital. It's time to tell Mac that Jenny is missing."

*B*renda bent down and kissed Mac. She smoothed his thick hair back and hesitated.

"What is it, Brenda? Do you know who did this to me?"

Tears filled her eyes and she wiped them away with the back of her hand. "I must tell you something, Mac." They locked eyes. "No one can locate Jenny. I've called her many times since your attack and she isn't answering." Mac shot up in bed. His hands went to his forehead in pain and she gently pushed him back down. "Don't do that, Mac. The doctors said to lie still."

"I can't just lie here and wonder about Jenny. I have to get out there and find her. Maybe she's back home now. Maybe her cell phone is dead. Did you try again?"

"Every officer who knows you is on this. Nothing will be

missed. She will turn up. You may be right about her cell phone going dead."

Brenda and Mac both knew that by now Jenny would have gone to Sheffield Bed and Breakfast if her phone didn't work or used the phone in her shop. She certainly would have gone to the police station and checked in with her father. Bryce will find her, thought Brenda fiercely. But she was scared that wasn't true. Was Bryce focused on Mac's attacker? Was the same person responsible for the petty thefts and Mac's assault and a possible kidnapping? It was too horrible to contemplate.

When Chief Bob Ingram entered the room, Brenda and Mac looked at him expectantly. He knew Brenda had told Mac about Jenny. He shook his head and sat next to the bed. "We will be up all night looking for her, Mac. You try to get some rest and let us do our work."

A nurse entered and told Mac it was time for his medication, handing him a pill that he swallowed. She informed him it would help ease the pain in his head. Brenda followed the nurse out into the hallway. "What was the pill really for?"

The nurse glanced toward the nurses' station. When she was satisfied no one could overhear her, she said. "It is to get him to relax. In other words, it's a mild sedative. The doctor doesn't want him to have a sleeping pill, just something to relax him so he will rest better until morning. He's agitated, and his heartrate has been elevated. If he doesn't get some rest, it will only take longer to heal the concussion."

The medication worked and Mac, though worried about his daughter, accepted that he couldn't physically do anything to help find her until he was discharged from the hospital. He finally sank back against his pillow, his eyes heavy-lidded with sleep. At last, Mac gave Brenda a wan smile as he drifted off to sleep.

The next morning, Brenda awoke in the easy chair she'd slept in. Mac looked surprised to see her there as he came awake in the early morning light. He chided her for trying to rest in a chair and told her to go home and sleep in her bed.

"I'm hoping you can come with me, Mac. I'll wait for the doctor's report on you today."

The pain had subsided in his head. Only a darkening bruise was visible and the color had begun to return to Mac's face. A tray that held his breakfast arrived and behind that, Chief Ingram came in.

"There's been another shop break-in," he told Mac. "Sweet Treats was vandalized early this morning. Hope said when she arrived at seven, she noticed the clock had fallen from the wall just inside the back door. It shattered when it fell, and the clock was stopped at six o'clock. It had to be this morning, since Hope didn't leave the shop until nine last night."

Mac groaned, this time from frustration, not pain. "I have to get out of here and back to work."

Bob and Brenda both knew he would heal faster if back at work. "If the doc says you can leave then you'll still have to go easy for a couple of days," the chief warned him. Mac nodded, silent.

An hour later, the doctor told Mac he could go home. "Don't go back to work as if nothing happened. Take it easy for a day or so and see how you feel."

The chief and Brenda exchanged glances. The three of them knew that wouldn't happen. Sweetfern Harbor needed all the help it could get.

"Let's go home first," Brenda said. "You'll need to freshen up and get some clean clothes."

"I'll get a shower and go from there." On the drive home, Brenda told him about the incident in the sitting room with the Wellingtons. They discussed the guests.

"I wonder about that photographer," Mac said. "He said he takes candid pictures at random. Is he really a photographer?"

Brenda told him she didn't do background checks on her guests, of course. "I know he came from Canada and is here to photograph the upcoming Winter Festival. It's against the law to run a background check without someone's permission, as you know. But perhaps Chief

Ingram can run a check on the guests, since they were all around during the time of your assault."

Brenda parked around the back of Sheffield Bed and Breakfast and they went in through the back door. She cautioned Mac to walk up the stairs slowly. They were on the back stairs and Brenda felt better using that way now that Mac was with her. The yellow crime scene tape had been removed from the stairs, though the closet where Mac had been discovered was sealed.

Mac's cell rang as they walked down the hallway to the apartment. Bryce told him they had not found Jenny yet but he and an officer were combing her house again for clues.

When Mac hung up, Brenda could see that he was worried for his daughter. She was worried that he might no longer think clearly regarding his own attack. While he showered, Brenda called Bryce. "I know Mac will get right back to work. Can you stick by his side when he gets to the police station? You are both going to give full attention to finding Jenny, so it won't be like you have to babysit him."

Bryce laughed for the first time since his fiancé's whereabouts had come into question. "I never think I'm babysitting my own boss. He will be an asset in finding Jenny. We'll leave nothing uncovered." When Brenda started to give him more advice, he assured her he would make sure Mac was all right during the workday ahead.

After his shower, Mac came out in clean clothes, running a towel over his hair. He told Brenda that it had to be a guest who attacked him. The back door was always locked and only someone with a key could enter. The front door was open only during business hours. No stranger would enter that way unless Allie or another staff member let someone in.

"Whoever attacked me is the one who has caused Jenny's disappearance. I'm sure of that." Brenda had drawn the same conclusion.

Excited voices drifted upstairs. At the top of the steps, they looked down to see Phyllis and William in the foyer. Brenda left Mac alone and raced down the steps to hug Phyllis.

"I'm so glad you two are back. We have a lot of catching up to do."

"Mac was attacked and now Jenny is missing," Allie said worriedly.

Phyllis and William answered with shocked faces.

"I guess we'll catch up quickly right now," Brenda said. She told them everything that had happened. Mac joined her and after assuring their friends he was fine, told them he was on his way to the police station to catch up on details. Then he planned to spend every minute looking for his daughter until she was found safe and sound. William told him he would take him down to the station.

William was well-known in Sweetfern Harbor and the surrounding area. He had ties with several people in high places. He kissed Phyllis and told her he would see her later.

After they left, she turned to Brenda. "Is Mac well enough to go back to work so soon?"

"He doesn't know it, but I put Bryce in charge of sticking by his side to make sure he stays safe and doesn't overwork himself. He's determined and we're all so worried about Jenny."

Since Allie didn't mention anything about the break-in at her mother's shop, Brenda told her about Sweet Treats and reassured Allie that her mother was fine. David, her father, was at the shop taking inventory to see if anything had been stolen, along with the cops.

"Call your mother in a few minutes and if she needs you there, go on down. We can handle things here. No one is checking out today and no more guests are expected, since we have a full house."

"I want to grab some things from my apartment, Brenda," Phyllis said. "I'll get everything out sometime this week and get moved completely in with William."

"I want you to keep the apartment, Phyllis. There may be some nights when you and William will want to stay here." She hadn't asked Phyllis if a replacement was needed. With William's wealth, she knew her housekeeper wouldn't have to work. She had a pang in her heart to think of losing her live-in best friend.

"If you're wondering, I'd like to keep my job here, Brenda. Unless you have hired someone else, of course," Phyllis said.

Brenda hugged her. "I haven't done that at all. We'll talk later, but right now I will go with you and chat while you pick up whatever you need."

Brenda told Phyllis everything about the recent events in more detail. They decided to go downtown and look at Jenny's Blossoms for possible clues. Brenda quickly drove them downtown and was relieved to think she might help move the investigation forward, finally.

A young officer was removing the tape from around the property just as they arrived. Brenda used the key that Jenny had given her for emergencies and they went inside. The display window remained in shambles, though it had been covered over with a sheet of plywood to keep the snow out. Silently, both women started to clean it up. They salvaged some of the winter display and Phyllis managed to reconstruct it, though not back to its perfectly detailed state that Jenny had arranged it in. Brenda swept the last debris into a dustbin when something in the corner of the display platform caught her eye.

It was the same type of paper with a typed message on it,

just like the one found at the bed and breakfast. She unfolded it completely and read it aloud. "Detective Mac Rivers can now pay for putting me behind bars. I lost everything. He will lose his daughter and know what that feels like."

The women looked at one another. Reality hit them. Jenny was in grave danger. Without words, they hurried to the car and left for the police station.

Mac and Bryce were climbing into their squad car in the station's parking lot. Just then, the screeching of tires on concrete caught their attention. Mac was startled to see Brenda's car pulling to a halt. Brenda ran to them and handed the note to Mac, explaining where it had been found. Mac looked half dazed and half enraged, but he kept his temper in check.

"It could be Sleazy," Bryce jumped in, realizing Mac was at a loss for words. When asked, he explained to the women the man's real name was Robert Waters. "He kidnapped two women and tied them up. He was ready to stab one when the other got loose and jumped on his back. She was a Karate instructor and knew what she was doing. Waters was left with a slash from his own knife on his left hand. Mac and another officer tracked him down. He spent time in jail."

"Surely he's still there," Phyllis said.

"No. He spent time in prison but the judge let him out early because of good behavior."

"And because jails are already overcrowded," Mac finally spoke up. "We can't be sure it's Robert Waters. If it is him, it couldn't be the same person who attacked me since he doesn't work there and he isn't a guest, for sure."

"I'm going to do some detective work of my own," Brenda said.

"I'm going with you," Phyllis said.

"The two of you be careful. We can use all the help available," Mac said, "but watch your backs." The two detectives had their own investigative trails to follow, and quickly departed in their squad car.

"Let's go to Jenny's house first," Brenda said. It was sobering to realize that they now had proof that the vandalism and petty thieveries around town were connected to Jenny's disappearance.

The house Mac once shared with his daughter looked the same as usual. Evidently the police officers who had stopped by earlier had crossed the lawn to the front door. Brenda could see their boot tracks leading to and from the curb to the door. Light snow covered the tracks that Jenny's car made leading into the garage. Brenda decided someone must have halted her before she had time to open the garage door. Her suspicions were confirmed when she saw scuff marks in the snow at the driver's side of the car.

"We can go inside," Brenda said. "Bryce told me the entire place has already been searched for clues."

Phyllis knew that the police didn't always pick up every clue. That's where Brenda's expertise came in. She rarely missed the small details of a crime scene. Phyllis noticed this same trait when Brenda examined her bed and breakfast before special events and before guests arrived. Everything was looked at with meticulous care. That's why Phyllis had faith that her boss and friend would find something the cops had overlooked.

However, Brenda found nothing but frustration inside the house. After going through every room, Brenda turned up nothing of significance. They went back outside and Brenda stooped down and examined the scuff marks again. The boot prints were almost covered over with new snow. Indications of two sets were obvious enough to know one set was Jenny's and the other someone with a larger shoe size. But that was where the trail went cold. Jenny's car was gone, and so was she, seemingly without a trace.

"I'm ready for a coffee break," Brenda said with a sigh. "Let's head for Morning Sun Coffee."

Phyllis smiled to her friend. "I'd better get down there anyway. Molly will be upset if I don't show up soon."

Phyllis was eager to reassure her daughter Molly that she was home safe, but she knew Brenda had more reasons than a cup of hot coffee to go to the coffee shop. Molly Lindsey's shop was the main meeting place for town gossip.

CHAPTER SIX

GUESTS

When they entered Morning Sun Coffee, voices buzzed louder than usual. Molly raced toward her mother and hugged her. When she stood back, they saw her stricken face smeared with dried tears. Fresh tears flowed again.

"Have they found Jenny yet?" Molly asked. Brenda shook her head no.

Marilyn Martin heard her question when she and Richard came in. "She will be found soon. I take it you and the detective's daughter are close friends?"

Molly nodded, unable to speak. Richard's eyes drifted around the shop until they rested on the crown moldings and then to the door. Brenda felt out of sorts already and lost patience with him for some reason she couldn't explain to herself.

"Are you looking for anything in particular?" she asked Richard.

Richard jerked to reality and smiled at her. "I'm just interested in Sweetfern Harbor's architecture. This shop in particular has unique moldings. I'm impressed."

Marilyn seemed exasperated with her husband but refrained from speaking to him about his answer which she felt was out of context to the events going on around them.

Moments later when a flash illuminated the shop, Brenda didn't have to question who entered. She glared at Philip Turner, who snapped photos right and left. A few customers posed for him. He went to the counter where Molly had returned to wait on her customers. Brenda walked to him and stood to his left. His hand rested on the counter while he waited for an espresso.

A long scar marred his strong hands. The fact that his nails were perfectly manicured was inconsequential next to the shock of seeing the ugly scar.

"How did you get that awful scar on your hand?" Brenda asked, forgetting her irritation with his photography.

Philip shrugged. "Several years ago I got into a fight with someone trying to steal my prized camera. I almost won except for the knife he had in his hand. The slash worked to deter me from fighting more." He laughed. "I was lucky to get away with my camera intact when a cop on the beat showed up."

"That must have been some fight," Brenda said. She wanted to keep the conversation going to give her time to study his features.

"It was. I had no idea at all he had a knife on him, until he slashed me." Philip seemed distracted by the photography opportunities in the café and quickly picked up his espresso and moved on, wishing Brenda a good day.

Phyllis and Brenda decided to return to Sheffield Bed and Breakfast. Brenda told her to pay close attention to guests who came in for lunch. Phyllis was glad to be in on the mystery of who was out to get Mac and his daughter. They hoped someone would say something that would hint as to where Jenny Rivers could be located.

As it turned out, only a few guests were at the bed and breakfast during lunch and no one said or did anything remotely suspicious. After lunch, Phyllis left to go to her apartment and retrieve needed items while Brenda checked on Allie, who told her that her parents were fine. David had left his wife at Sweet Treats to complete cleanup and plans for the Winter Festival. Allie planned to practice her skating routine after work, which told Brenda that her young reservationist was not terribly disturbed by the events of the past couple days.

"I overheard a conversation earlier after you and Phyllis left," Allie said. She told Brenda about hearing Thomas Wellington on the phone. "I didn't eavesdrop. Anyone could have heard him."

Brenda prodded her to continue. Allie told her that after the call where he seemed to talk of some kind of business plan, his wife approached him and asked if things were going to work out. Thomas told Rachel things were going along well and to have no worries.

"I hope it does work out. I thought they came here for a getaway," Brenda said. "I guess whatever business deal that followed him here can finally allow that."

Allie shook her head. "I think it's more than some business deal. Something about the tone of voice was a little strange."

Brenda tried to reassure Allie, but inwardly she had been suspicious of the Wellingtons, especially after the sitting room scene the other night. She knew she would keep a much closer eye on them for the next few days before the Winter Festival began.

Mac arrived home late and stretched across the bed. Brenda was glad to see him rest but noted he was pale. She wanted to admonish him for overdoing it but withheld her opinion. He already knew that. "Try and get some sleep, Mac."

"I will, but first tell me if you found out anything at all today that will lead us to Jenny. Anything, Brenda."

Brenda told him of the quirks she noticed with Richard Martin at the coffee shop, of the overheard conversation between the Wellingtons, and then about Philip Turner and his scar. Mac sat up and listened to her description.

"Other than the scar on his hand, nothing you describe about him makes me think he is Sleazy," Mac said. "Robert Waters' physique is similar to his, but other than that, he doesn't look like him in the least. The scar, I believe, is coincidental, I'm afraid."

"I wish I had more, Mac."

Mac slept for a couple of hours and then got up and changed clothes. When she asked, he told Brenda he was going back down to the police station to go over everything found so far.

"I must find Jenny before I can rest easy again." He kissed Brenda. "I'm just wondering why whoever is responsible hasn't demanded anything in return from me." He grew somber. "I guess he has demanded, after all. He does have Jenny or has done something to her to hurt me. But who is it, Brenda?" She knew he didn't expect an answer from her. "I'll be at the station in about fifteen minutes. I'll call you when I'm in my office, so you won't worry."

On the third step down in the back stairwell, Mac bent to pick up another note on identical paper. "Jenny is safe for now, but if necessary I will kill her and you too for putting me behind bars." Tracing the source of the paper was in the works already and it was a matter of the waiting game. Frustratingly, there was no mention of what the kidnapper meant by "if necessary." Mac set off for the station with renewed energy.

Brenda called Bryce to tell him Mac returned to his office. Bryce was at Jenny's house and told Brenda he would go right down and help out.

"I have to find her, Brenda. I can't live without her." Brenda caught tears in his voice. Neither detective could manage sleep. Brenda decided they were better off working the case, so close to home.

"She will come home to you and all of us, Bryce. The best detectives are on it."

Brenda glanced at the clock, which read eleven. There was no going back to sleep for her either at this point. She headed downstairs in search of a sweet roll and more tea bags to replenish her stash. While heating water in the kitchen, she heard the front door open. The hushed voices of Marilyn and Richard Martin echoed down the hall and made their way to the open kitchen door.

"I'm going to take a quick stroll around the grounds before bed."

"You can't seem to get enough of this bitter cold, Richard. Make it a fast walk and I'll have the fire going in our fireplace."

Brenda turned the kitchen light off and waited for Richard to circle around to the back of the house. She looked twice to determine if she was imagining things when she saw a light flashing from the wooded area. Then it waved from side to side, as if signaling Richard. The next moment, she observed someone emerging from the tree line to meet Richard. The person was shadowed and Brenda failed to recognize the person. She walked to the back door and opened it gently. For certain, Richard Martin is one of the men. She turned around when someone else entered the front door.

William spotted her first down the hallway and waved. "We're back for Phyllis' wool sweater she wanted. Then we're homeward bound." Brenda hurried to them.

She told them what she witnessed in the backyard. William walked quickly to the back door. Inadvertently, he allowed the storm door to slam. The figure at the tree line disappeared back into the woods. Richard waved at William, as if out for a midnight stroll.

If the figure in the woods had stuck around a little longer, he would have seen law enforcement arriving at the bed and breakfast. As it turned out, he ran as fast as he could and the woods swallowed him up in the darkness of the night. He made his way into the local tavern and ordered a beer.

Richard made his way confidently through the dark, snowy yard to the door as if nothing had happened. "Thanks for opening the door for me, William. It is William, isn't it? I heard you and the housekeeper were getting back in town. I'm Richard Martin, one of the guests."

William held his tongue. Phyllis was much more than a housekeeper in his eyes. She was his beloved and loving wife and it irked him that a guest would refer to her like a servant. He decided to return cordiality.

"Let's go down to the sitting room and have a nightcap," William insisted. "I always like to meet new people. I hear you're a history buff."

As they came down the hallway, Brenda could not contain her curiosity. She asked Richard who he was talking to outside at this time of night. At first he denied he was talking with anyone until Brenda pressed him further. He then told her he met up with someone he knew a long time ago. Brenda had many more questions to ask but caught a quick warning look from William.

"Richard and I are going to grab a nightcap and get to know one another better. Would you like one, Brenda?"

Brenda attempted a smile. "Thanks, but I have my hot tea and will call it a night."

While William occupied Richard, Brenda called Mac. In no time at all, the two detectives arrived at Sheffield Bed and Breakfast and went into the sitting room. Richard stood up and spoke first.

"It looks like you'll have more company to finish your nightcap, William. I'm going to turn in before my wife comes looking for me." He turned to William and smiled. "Your expertise on local architecture has been most interesting. Thank you."

Mac stepped forward while Bryce stood guard at the doorway. "We are here to talk with you, Richard. Not many people unfamiliar with our area take strolls out in this weather in the middle of the night. Why did you do that?"

Richard's eyes darted from the floor to the ceiling and finally landed on the detective's face. "I enjoy night walks in cold weather. I always sleep better after a brisk walk."

"Do you always meet up with someone you haven't seen in years during your midnight walks?"

Richard's eyes shifted again. "It's true that I did run into someone I knew quite a while ago." Mac's eyebrows shot higher. "I didn't expect to see anyone back there at this time of night."

"As I understand it, the person you met signaled his presence to you and you followed his direction. Was that also coincidental?"

Richard looked as if he was ready to bolt but knew better than to try and escape. Odds were he wouldn't make it out of the room. "All right, Detective. I knew, like everyone else around here, that your daughter is missing. I arranged to meet the man near the trees because I was told he had information on her whereabouts. He was getting ready to tell me who knocked you out, too, just as William came to the door." For a split second he displayed a look of pity toward Mac. "I guess that information is lost on all of us now."

Mac knew that only law enforcement, the Pendletons, Chef Morgan, and Brenda knew of the attack on him. All had been sworn to secrecy about it.

"Do you have a name for this informant?"

Bryce stood firm, waiting for the man to try and escape. William had stood up with his back to the door that led to the dining area as he watched the proceedings. Brenda stood out in the hallway listening, and out of sight. She slipped into the alcove, closed the door and called for back-up with no sirens.

"My informant is a guest here. His name is Thomas Wellington. At least that's the name he tells everyone. He's really Neb Tyler."

Bryce spoke for the first time. "Are you talking about Neb Tyler, the bank robber who kidnapped that teller in his getaway with Robert Waters?"

"You are lying," Mac said. "Thomas Wellington looks nothing like Neb Tyler."

Richard shook his head vigorously. "I swear the man you think is Thomas Wellington is Neb Tyler, the bank robber." At this point, Richard didn't hold back, wanting to prove himself. "He told me he knows where Jenny is. I can prove he is the same man. He told me a while back that he robbed the bank because he and his wife were dirt poor and needed money. I know you are the one who nabbed him, Detective Rivers. He didn't mean harm during that bank robbery but he took the teller because he had to ensure his escape. He and his wife just needed money to live on."

"All that you are telling me, except for his excuses, is public knowledge."

"Did you know he once had a daughter the same age as your daughter? You were the one who caught him just at the city limits and were responsible for his conviction and incarceration. He loved his daughter like you love yours and you took her away from him. He said he planned for years how to make you pay. He didn't want to kill you. He wanted you to suffer like he did, without your daughter. He knocked you unconscious to keep you from your daughter while she

71

was being taken. Don't you get it, Detective? He wanted you to pay."

Mac knew that Neb's daughter was mentioned only once in the news reports during the ongoing investigation. It was Family Protective Services that took her from her parents. Still, the man he met as a guest at Sheffield Bed and Breakfast looked nothing at all like Neb Tyler.

Bryce glanced toward the front door when Brenda opened it for the swarm of officers who flooded into the hallway.

"We have back-up here, Mac," Bryce said.

Mac stood back as Bryce took out his handcuffs in front of Richard Martin. "I have a lot more questions for you to answer, Richard," he told the suspect. "You can make this easy, or you can make this hard." Richard Martin clenched his jaw and offered his wrists to be handcuffed. Bryce told the officers he would follow them down to the police station right away.

When he returned to the sitting room, Bryce demanded to know why Mac hadn't pressed Richard as to where Jenny was being kept. "I need to get to her. Who knows where this Thomas Wellington is now?"

Brenda looked at Mac. "I checked upstairs—Thomas Wellington isn't here right now."

Mac nodded and turned to Bryce. "I want you to go right

now to the station and start interrogating Richard. Something isn't right about everything he said," said Mac, shaking his head. "If it is Neb impersonating someone by the name of Thomas Wellington, then who really left me unconscious and took Jenny? There is more than one person involved. Take fingerprints of Wellington before anything else. I'll get to Jenny."

Mac pulled Brenda to him. "Before this night ends, we will have Jenny home safe and sound."

Detective Jones sped to the police station and jogged into the building. He barked orders regarding fingerprints. The night clerk told him it was being done and pointed out which interrogation room the suspect would be taken to. Bryce waited for the two officers to process Richard Martin as Chief Ingram watched. Bryce glared at Richard Martin and then joined the Chief across from him at the interrogation room table.

"I'm told the man you connected with is Neb Tyler. I am also told he looks nothing like the bank robber," the chief said. He leaned back, perusing the file in front of him. "So who did you talk with tonight in the cold?"

"Like I said, I talked with Neb Tyler. You've heard of plastic surgery, haven't you, Chief?"

Bob Ingram jerked forward. His eyes were steel as they bored into the man's face. There was a knock on the door and Mac was allowed inside. He sat next to Bryce, who couldn't wait any longer.

"Where's Jenny Rivers?" he asked the man.

Richard Martin smiled. "What's in it for me?" He looked from Mac to Bryce.

Chief Ingram ignored his question. "Where is she? Do you really have any information at all? Did you really see Neb Tyler? When he finally got out of prison he left for Montana. We keep tabs on people like him."

Richard chuckled as if fully in control. "Apparently not, or you would know he's right here in Sweetfern Harbor."

It was going to be a long night.

After the police left with Richard in custody, Brenda wanted to talk to Marilyn Martin. She knocked softly on her door. Marilyn opened the door with a smile on her face, a glass of wine in her hand and a low burning fire in the fireplace behind her. When she saw that it was Brenda, her demeanor changed to one of embarrassment.

"I'm sorry, Brenda, I was sure it was Richard. I promised him a warm welcome when he finished his ridiculously cold winter walk." She leaned her head around Brenda. "Where is he? He's been gone for quite some time."

"He won't be back tonight." Brenda asked if she could come inside the room. Marilyn stood back and Brenda closed the door behind her. She explained that Marilyn's husband had been taken to the police station for interrogation.

"Interrogation? Whatever for?" Marilyn asked. Her eyes grew wide and luminous with unshed tears. "What has he done? I didn't think a walk around the grounds was something criminal."

"He told the police he met up with someone outside who knows where Mac's daughter is. She was kidnapped, as we are learning now. He could be arrested for being accessory to the crime. Do you know anything about that?"

"Of course I knew Detective Rivers' daughter was missing. Everyone we met in town talked about it. What does that have to do with my husband?" Marilyn held her breath and hoped the answer didn't incriminate Richard in any way, though she couldn't imagine why it would.

"If he met up with someone who knows where she is, then he is deeply involved for that alone. Do you know Thomas and Rachel Wellington?"

"I met them when we came here a few days ago. Until then I had never met them at all. Are they involved in this somehow?"

"There are a lot of unknowns at this point." Brenda asked Marilyn to tell her how she met and married Richard.

"We met about eight years ago through a mutual friend. My sister warned me against marrying him. She thought there was something not right about him. I told her if I was his third wife it simply meant he hadn't found the right one until I came along."

She wrung her hands after placing the glass of wine on the end table. "We've had a wonderful marriage until the last year or so. I don't know what's going on with Richard, but he has become more and more distant toward me. I thought coming here was a great idea to rekindle our marriage. He came up with the plan and that really made me feel good, that we were going to be all right after all. As it turns out, he hasn't shown me much attention since we arrived."

Brenda made mental notes of the information Marilyn gave her. Suddenly, Marilyn stood up and paced back and forth.

"I can't believe he's in jail. What will happen and what will I tell anyone who asks where he is?"

"He may not stay there tonight. It depends on what information they find out from him. Just tell everyone he's out early and will be gone all day if he has to stay there a while."

Brenda felt sure Richard would be spending the night in

jail and probably more than one night. She left Marilyn convinced the woman didn't really know her husband at all.

Everyone else in the bed and breakfast was sound asleep. Thomas had not returned, if he was even out in the woods to begin with. No lights filtered from under the doorways along the passageway. Brenda found it impossible to sleep knowing Jenny was out there somewhere. She was probably miserable and scared. She spent the next few hours going over everything Richard said in the sitting room and thought about the other guests. According to Richard, it was Thomas Wellington who knocked Mac unconscious, but for some reason Mac had his doubts. The last time Brenda looked at the clock, it read two in the morning before she finally fell into a deep sleep with no answers.

After hours of fruitless questioning, Mac motioned for the chief and Bryce to come out into the hallway to talk. They left Richard in the room alone with cameras on him.

"I'm going to try to find Thomas Wellington. I have a feeling he's not asleep at the bed and breakfast," Mac said.

"I'm coming with you," Bryce said.

Bob Ingram knew his detectives well enough not to argue. After all, if the missing person was his daughter or his fiancé, he'd be desperate for answers, too. He took another officer back into the room to begin another round of questioning with Richard Martin.

"Where are we going first?" Bryce asked as he followed Mac out to the parking lot.

"We're going to cruise the streets and look for his SUV. He's driving an Escape, according to Brenda. It's a deep grey color. If we don't see it, then we're going into any business still open this time of night."

Bryce looked at his watch. "That would be the tavern then. They'll be closing in half an hour. Shouldn't we go there first?"

"We will after we cruise down the alleys behind all the shops. Look for anything unusual. Then we'll head for the bar if necessary."

"Do you think he's Neb Tyler?"

"It could be. The physique matches, but not the looks or hair color. He could have undergone plastic surgery but it would have to have been expensive and a complete job."

The streets and alleys were empty except for a few parked cars belonging to people who lived over businesses in downtown Sweetfern Harbor. They neared the Octopus Tavern.

Bryce pointed. "Is that him?"

"That's Thomas Wellington for sure. Let's go."

The officers got out of the patrol car and walked briskly toward the slightly inebriated man coming from the bar. He saw the two cops and ran. Bryce chased him until he caught up with him. Mac was on his heels.

"What are you running from, Thomas, or is it Neb?" Mac asked.

Expletives exploded from the man's mouth as Bryce jerked him around and snapped handcuffs on him. He shoved him into the back of the patrol car and they headed for the police station.

Chief Ingram came from the interrogation room. He smiled to himself when he saw the two officers come in with the suspect.

"That was quick work," he said. "This is Thomas Wellington, I take it?"

"That's who he says he is. He ran from us when he saw us," Bryce said. "He staggered out of Octopus Tavern."

Bryce pushed him toward the booking counter, where he couldn't wait to get the fingerprints of the man. If he was responsible for the disappearance of Jenny, then she was all right where she was since Thomas, or Neb, as well as Richard were in custody. The detective's adrenaline raced. Any minute now he would be on his way to rescue the woman he loved so much.

"Fingerprints will tell us if this man is Neb Tyler." The chief agreed with Mac. "I'm not leaving tonight until one or both of them tell us where Jenny is. I have to find her." The chief nodded.

The officers didn't spend time wondering about Neb's changed appearance, if that was indeed who they had in their hands. Bryce spent his time hovering over the shoulder of the tech while she ran the fingerprints. She felt his hot breath on her neck and turned to glare at him.

"I'll have them as soon as possible. If he's who you think he is, they will match since he's been in prison before." She paused as she waited for the detective to step back. Then the printout erupted from the printer and Bryce grabbed it before she had a chance to hand it to him. When he raced from the room, she said aloud, "I guess you got what you wanted."

Mac and Bob turned when the straight-backed chair in the narrow hallway tumbled over. The young detective didn't bother to upright it. "It's him. It's Neb Tyler."

"I'll send officers to the bed and breakfast to get his wife down here," the chief said. "That means Rachel Wellington is really Rachel Tyler. She's been in on things with him before, even though we never had tangible proof."

In the meantime, the two suspects sat alone in their interrogation rooms. Mac called Brenda to alert her. She dressed quickly and walked on tiptoe down to the foyer to wait for the arresting officers to arrive. She barely had time enough to regret the fact that her bed and breakfast housed criminals. When the cops arrived, she told them to follow her to Rachel's door. As far as she knew, Rachel slept. She was right about that.

The woman's eyes opened at the sound of the heavy knock. She glanced at her watch on the nightstand and felt for Thomas. He had not slept in the bed and it was early in the morning. She imagined him dead drunk in some alley, knowing he was on edge about their deeds. A drink or two usually calmed him down but he must have had more than a few.

"Who is it?" she called.

Then she heard the key in the lock and Brenda stepped inside the room after flicking on the overhead light. A female officer stepped around Brenda and told Rachel she was under arrest for suspicion of aiding her husband in the kidnapping of Jenny Rivers. Rachel was silent. The officers allowed Rachel to get dressed and then handcuffed her without incident. Brenda was thankful everyone else slept peacefully through it all.

The familiar twisting of fingers started until handcuffs were snapped in place. Rachel's eyes filled with trepidation when she passed Brenda. When they all left,

Brenda finished getting ready to face a long day and headed for the police station. She wanted to listen to more interrogations and to hear what Rachel had to say.

Above all, she wanted to be there to hear where Jenny was being held, and to rescue her.

CHAPTER EIGHT

CRIMINAL ACTIVITY

*B*renda went into the police station and asked which room Neb Tyler was in. The clerk told her and Chief Ingram to meet her at the one-way window in the hallway.

"If you want, Brenda, you can sit in on the interrogation. Jenny is your daughter, too." Bob looked at her carefully when he spoke the words. "If you think it will upset you too much, take it only as an offer. I know you are anxious like the rest of us to find her."

"I do want to sit in there and look at him eye to eye. I had no idea I housed criminals. I can't believe they would pretend to be my guests and then commit crimes like this. I'm sick to my stomach over it."

The chief paused, seeing her distress. "None of this is

your fault, Brenda. Criminals aren't known for their honesty. How could you have known?"

Brenda barely smiled. "I know you are right. We all commented on how much time Thomas Wellington spent on the phone about business. Who knew it was criminal business all along?" She brushed her hair back with her right hand. "Have they said anything to Mac as to why they took Jenny?"

Chief Ingram explained one or both came up with the idea to punish Mac. "The notes indicate one had his family taken away when he went to prison and wanted Mac to see how that felt."

Brenda shuddered. "Let's get this going. You can rely on me to keep quiet. I want to observe and listen to what Neb has to say."

Bob Ingram smiled to himself. It would be something if Brenda Sheffield Rivers held back from asking pointed questions. Mac joined them. The chief told Bryce to observe from the window and they would call him in halfway through. The young detective was too emotionally involved and the chief didn't want him riled up, trying to force confessions. Bryce wasn't happy about having to stand on the sidelines. The chief told him it would give him time to calm down and think rationally.

Just before opening the door, Brenda stopped her

husband and the chief. "Do we know who actually planned things?"

"That's what we'll find out," Mac said. "First of all, we'll make sure one or the other tells us where Jenny is."

Brenda took a deep breath and went into the room. Neb Tyler's demeanor was one of anger and resentment. He glared at Mac until he noticed Brenda. "What's she doing here?" His voice snarled like a wild animal.

The chief stopped the prisoner before he had a chance to object further. "You are in no position to question anything right now. That includes who comes into this room and who doesn't."

Mac started to read his rights to him. Neb waved his hand back and forth. "I've heard all of that from you on the street. I don't need to hear it again."

No one reminded the man he could ask for a lawyer. He didn't seem interested in doing so anyway. Brenda thought that meant he didn't plan to give out any information to anyone in the room.

"From the notes you left around, we know you have Jenny." Mac moved forward to stare down the man. "Was that your idea or did you have help?" Neb didn't correct Mac that it was Richard Martin who left the notes. He cocked his head, looking at the detectives. That piece of information could remain a mystery for the time being. The cat and mouse game began.

Neb Tyler leaned back and shifted to a more comfortable stance. "I had help. It took some planning." This was more than Brenda expected. The man admitted to his part without much prodding. He smiled at Brenda. "You have a comfortable place. We had everything we needed and were waited on by your idiot staff like we were royalty."

Just as he sent the poisonous compliment her way, he turned to Mac. Anger washed over his eyes until they resembled black holes in his face. "It was because of you I was sent to not so luxurious accommodations in the past. You are the one who took what meant most to me and that was my own child. How does it feel to have yours taken away from you?"

Mac opened his mouth to answer. Chief Ingram interrupted before words actually left his mouth. "You put yourself there, Neb. You robbed yourself of your daughter. Neither Detective Rivers nor anyone else took anything from you." Another sneer was the only response. "Where is Jenny Rivers?"

Neb shrugged and remained silent. Brenda stood up. Everyone looked at her. She asked the chief and Mac to come outside the room with her. Bryce whipped around to meet them.

"Why are you leaving him so soon?" he demanded.

"Calm down, Bryce. I have an idea," Brenda said. She

went on to tell them she felt Richard Martin would be more cooperative in giving answers. "I'd like to interrogate him while you keep hammering at Neb. Bryce could join me. I think Richard will be ready to spill things in hopes it will benefit him in the long run."

The chief agreed and reminded Bryce to stay calm if they wanted to find out where Jenny was. "If you lose your cool, you may destroy all chances."

"I know that. I'll conduct myself as if this is another matter entirely."

Chief Ingram and Mac returned to Neb. They settled in, expecting a long interview day.

Brenda and Bryce passed the second window and noted Richard Martin bent over the table with his head in his hands. They entered the room. The surprised look on the man's face when he saw Brenda was a hint that he had been caught off-guard by something.

"How's Marilyn doing?" he stammered.

"She's fine, though deeply disappointed to hear you are in jail." Was that a flash of regret? Brenda wondered.

"We have to get to the bottom of things," Bryce said. "Tell us everything you know, from the beginning when you first met Neb Tyler."

"So you know the man is Neb for sure?" Neither Brenda nor Bryce answered him. "Okay, I'll tell you everything I know. I first met Neb when we played poker together in a nearby town. He seemed to be an all right guy and we saw one another on occasion. I guess he started to trust me enough to let me in on what kind of man he really is." He looked at the two across from him. "Can I have a drink of water?" Bryce motioned to the cop at the door who brought a bottle of water to Richard. They waited for him to continue.

"He had robbed a bank and kidnapped one of the tellers. He told me he and his wife Rachel were desperate for money. They had a kid by that time and no food to eat. That's why he robbed it. He spent the better part of his adult life in prison and his kid grew up without him. He never got over that part. Every day that passed he resented Detective Rivers more and more. His kid is about the age of the detective's daughter. I don't know where Neb's daughter is today, but I know she won't allow any contact. Neb wanted to teach the detective a lesson once he got out of prison and he told me all about it." Brenda felt Bryce tense up.

"The biggest question is where is Jenny being held?" Brenda didn't dare ask if she was alive or dead. She wanted to keep things on an even keel. Richard Martin appeared ready to talk and she didn't want to lose that momentum. Bryce got the message when she nudged him. Richard Martin seemed reluctant to answer the question, however, hesitating as he took a sip of his water.

"There's something off in your story about Neb Tyler," Bryce said. "He confessed to it, but he swore under oath he didn't plan that bank robbery alone. He had help." Bryce leaned back. "How did you manage to get away with it and only Neb went to prison?"

Brenda admired Bryce. He was more knowledgeable about Richard's and Neb's past lives than she was, or he was fabricating things to encourage Richard to tell more.

Richard shrugged his shoulders. "I got lucky. Okay, it's true I knew Neb before the robbery. We hadn't seen one another for years while he was in prison. When he got out, he looked me up and vowed to turn me in if I didn't help him take the detective's daughter. He said I owed him since he took the fall for the robbery and kidnapping. I had no choice."

"You had a choice. You could have warned Detective Rivers before you acted." Bryce simmered quietly. "Kidnapping is a serious felony offense. Neb was lucky some judge let him out long before he was due, just for good behavior. Are you two responsible for all the shop robberies around town?"

Richard nodded his head yes and wiped his brow with the back of his hand. "We did that as a trial run to see how sharp your police force was. Each one was a little worse, a little more risky. When we did Jenny's shop successfully, Neb said it was time to go to the next step in the plan. You were getting outside help involved and we didn't want to get caught before Neb could finish the job he came to do."

By this time, Brenda's adrenaline had increased until she was on the same level as Bryce. "Again, where is Jenny? You've nothing to lose at this point," she said.

"Listen, I only participated because I owed Neb something. He never turned me in and it was time for me to give back to him. She's alive even though he wanted me to kill her. I drew the line at murder." He was so caught up in his explanations he had no idea of how ludicrous this sounded to Bryce and Brenda.

"Which of you knocked Mac out on the back stairs?" Brenda asked, switching tacks. If she knew the assailant, she would know who kidnapped Jenny. It took two people to carry it all out, but they couldn't have been in the same place at the same time.

"I did," Richard said with a half-smile. "Neb typed up the notes and I placed them where he wanted them. He waited for Jenny to get home while I took care of Mac. We didn't want them trying to contact each other before we had her."

"You've confessed to everything. Now tell us where she is." Bryce had moved forward at the table, his knuckles white as he gripped the table. Richard's life was in his hands if he didn't tell them where Jenny was being kept.

"She's in a warm place. At least Neb said he turned on

that furnace down there. I'm not even sure there is a furnace in that fishing hut...I haven't seen her, but he told me she is still alive, though he's thinking of killing her himself..."

Bryce suddenly slammed one fist onto the surface of the table, startling Richard into silence. The detective seethed with impatience and his eyes burned into the man cowering across the table from him.

"Where is she?" Brenda repeated in a quiet tone.

Richard gave directions to the spot near the ocean where several fishing huts stood, eyeing Bryce carefully to make sure the detective didn't move towards him with those fists. "He put her in one that is empty all winter long. He told me it is the only one with a weathered grey door on it. That's all I know. I didn't take her there and I haven't seen her."

Before he finished his sentence, Bryce was at the door. He instructed the cop to take the prisoner to his cell and keep him there. Brenda raced after him. "Tell the chief we're on our way to get Jenny," Bryce told the clerk as they sprinted to the door.

Brenda buckled her seatbelt as Bryce, with sirens blaring, raced to the beach. They parked and ran to the row of six fishing huts. The weathered grey door was there, as described. All the other doors were shades of blue or brown. Bryce pulled the grey door open on its rusty hinges and light flooded into the dark interior. Brenda caught her breath when she saw Jenny. Her mouth was taped and wrists tied with a rough rope behind her back. Bryce carefully ripped the tape from his fiancé's mouth and kissed her long. The cabin was cold. Bryce shed his coat and wrapped it around Jenny while they worked to free her from the ropes. Brenda called Mac to give him the news. The chief had already sent patrol cars to the beach to secure it as a crime scene.

Things moved fast as police officers swarmed around the little cabin. Brenda finally spoke to Jenny. "Are you harmed, Jenny? Do you need an ambulance?"

"Oh, Brenda, I'm more than good now. I knew you would find me. I don't need an ambulance at all." Jenny's teeth chattered with cold but her eyes were bright as she spoke on. "It's been horrible not knowing what was going to happen to me." She looked at Bryce. "I was afraid I lost you forever, Bryce. That man had sheer meanness in his face. I thought he was going to kill me." He reached again for her and pulled her close.

"You need to get checked out, Jenny," Bryce said. "If you don't want an ambulance then we'll take you to the emergency room ourselves." Brenda agreed right away. She knew the full impact of Jenny's ordeal would only kick in once the relief of being found subsided.

Brenda called Mac to tell him Jenny was fine and to meet them at the hospital since she needed to be checked out.

Mac wouldn't feel easy about his daughter's wellbeing until he saw for himself, so he promised to finish up the interrogations and meet them there shortly. Brenda sat in the backseat as they drove and hugged Jenny close to her. The cold had settled in on her during the long captivity and she needed more warmth. Again Bryce put the sirens on until they arrived at the hospital for the much-needed examination.

Some time after she had been cleared by the doctors, everyone gathered around Jenny in her private room. She insisted she just needed to get home. "Other than the cold, I'm fine. I can't get better away from my loved ones."

Mac fully understood her desire. He agreed, but when she insisted on going back to her home, he objected. "You'll come to the bed and breakfast with us, Jenny. We have the pull-out sofa in our apartment and you can recover right there. Besides, we'll have a lot of questions to ask you about your ordeal and you'll be more comfortable with us."

Bryce had other ideas of his own but saved them for now. He knew Mac was right. Jenny didn't need to go home to an empty house and to where it all began for her. Bryce's own apartment was a studio apartment over a shop downtown with little room to move freely. His mind raced with his thoughts. He knew what he wanted to do but would give Jenny time first.

At Sheffield Bed and Breakfast, word had already

reached everyone that Jenny was found alive and well. Phyllis had a tray of homemade oatmeal raisin cookies and hot tea waiting for them all. She gathered soft quilts ready to wrap Jenny in. Allie called her parents, and shortly after, Hope and David Williams arrived to welcome Jenny home as well. Molly Lindsey burst into the bed and breakfast and demanded to know where her best friend was.

"Calm down, Molly," said her mother. "I've got hot tea and cookies ready. She will be here as soon as possible. William met all of them at the hospital. He said he saw her with his own eyes. She is fine but exhausted. They should be here any minute."

CHAPTER NINE

HOMECOMING

The waiting seemed endless though only minutes passed. Everyone chatted animatedly in the sitting room about the recovery of Jenny Rivers as well as the upcoming festival. Molly finally calmed down at her mother's encouragement and joined the others in the sitting room. They had settled in chairs and on the loveseat just as Mac's car drove up, followed by Bryce and Jenny. William sat next to Mac. Jenny clung to Bryce's arm as he helped her inside to greet her friends. Everyone cried tears of joy. Phyllis ordered Jenny to curl up on the loveseat and then she proceeded to wrap the softest quilt around her. Brenda poured hot tea and handed the cup to Jenny. William and Bryce busied themselves stoking up the fire in the hearth so that it burned bright and hot.

"It's so good to be out of that awful fishing shack," she told them.

"I don't know how you managed to keep your sanity," Molly said. "I would have been so scared."

"I was scared at first, but then I spent time trying to figure how I would escape if that awful man came back. Overall, it wasn't too hard since I knew Bryce or Brenda or my dad would find me soon. They are all the best and I am more than thankful I was found before I froze to death." She laughed. "The rope was tight and I couldn't loosen it enough, even though I tried more than once." She rubbed her wrists.

"We're thankful you are home safe and sound," Phyllis said. William stood by her and put his arm around his wife's shoulders.

"I hope the person who did this can be found soon." Hope's worried look reminded the officers and Brenda that no one knew the final details.

"There are two men in custody right now. They are charged with attacking me and with taking Jenny. They aren't going anywhere any time soon," Mac said. "All of you can rest assured our town is safe again."

"They have charges of burglaries against them, too," Bryce said. "They won't see the light of day for a long time yet."

Allie left the room to answer the phone. After the call, she started back into the sitting room when she saw a tearful guest coming down with her luggage. Marilyn Martin told her she was checking out.

"I'm sure Brenda won't want me to stay around." Allie looked puzzled. "My husband is one of the criminals charged with taking Jenny Rivers."

Allie opened her mouth but couldn't think of words to say. Recovering, she finally spoke. "Wait right here. I'll get Brenda."

When Brenda came out, Mac was with her. "I'm checking out, Brenda. I called and one of the local motels has a room. I'm sure I'll be expected to stick around for more questioning," said Marilyn.

Mac agreed they would need to talk with her and he got the information from her in regard to her location plans. Brenda looked at the woman. She was sure Marilyn Martin didn't participate in any crimes with her husband but understood there was no proof of that yet. She debated as to whether she should insist the woman remain where she was or not.

"It is your choice, Marilyn." Brenda looked at Mac. His look told her not to take a chance. "I understand if you want to go elsewhere."

"To be truthful," Marilyn said, "I'm not sure of our money situation right now. There are so many unknowns with Richard that I should probably find more economical lodging for now." She thanked Brenda for her hospitality at the historic Queen Anne bed and breakfast. Brenda felt relief that she chose to leave and watched as her guest departed.

When they returned to the sitting room, everyone talked about the Winter Festival. "We have less than two days before things begin," Molly said.

Brenda saw that Jenny appeared very tired. "We'll get on with plans for that right after Jenny gets a good night's sleep."

It was her remark that drew everyone's attention back to Jenny. Her face had paled since her arrival and dark circles formed under her eyes. Molly hugged her tightly and told her again how happy she was to see her home safe and sound. One by one the others did the same. Only Phyllis and William Pendleton remained where they were. Allie had finished for the day and left to practice her ice skating routine for the competition. Bryce clung to Jenny as if she was going to disappear again. Her eyes filled with deep love for him. Now was the time, he thought.

He told her to stay right where she was. "I have something to say to you, Jenny." Everyone remaining in the room turned to watch with expectation. "I know we set our wedding date for the summer, but I want to marry you much sooner. There is no reason for you to live alone in that big house."

"What are you saying, Bryce?" Jenny's eyes danced.

"I want to marry you right away, perhaps as soon as the Winter Festival is over, or we can marry as soon as you want. I don't want you to have to live in fear, thinking of possible criminals lurking around or any other unsafe thoughts that could plague you after what you've been through. I want you to feel safe."

"I like the idea of marrying sooner, but you don't have to worry about me living alone until then. Remember, I have lived with a father who was always out and about in the middle of the night because of something criminal going on around town. I'm a grown woman, I don't want you to worry about me."

Mac stepped forward. "It's true I've had to leave her in the middle of the night like that, but I want to remind everyone that when she was younger, after her mother died, Jenny's nanny Natalie was there with her." It was true the woman had cared for her like a mother.

"That's right. I don't want anyone to get the wrong idea, he didn't leave me alone as a kid," Jenny laughed. Father and daughter exchanged loving smiles.

Bryce realized they were veering from the topic at hand. "I meant what I said, Jenny. I want to marry you as soon as possible and we all heard you agree to that."

Jenny laughed. "Of course I'm ready to marry you, Bryce. But I hope you aren't doing it under the delusion that it will somehow keep me safe. We have to do it for all the right reasons."

"All right, then, Jenny, I want to marry you right now because I can't live without you and because I love you deeply. I want to make you completely mine as soon as possible. What happened to you brought it home more than ever how much I love you."

That was the longest and most heartfelt speech anyone in the room had heard come from the young detective's mouth. Brenda marveled inwardly at how brash and flirtatious he had been when she first met him. She realized Philip Turner had the same personality. The photographer was just as cavalier as Bryce Jones had been when he first arrived in Sweetfern Harbor. Both men were flirts. Bryce, however, had matured into a fine young man.

A moment passed as the lovebirds held hands. Everything had been said that needed saying and Bryce embraced Jenny again. They kissed long, until the two newlywed couples turned and left them alone. Phyllis and Brenda exchanged knowing smiles as they closed the sitting room door behind them.

William stated they needed to get home and get settled in. Phyllis promised Brenda she would come back and dig in on preparations for hosting the end of the festivities.

"I'm sure there is a lot still to be done, Brenda." Brenda assured her there was.

Mac stuck his head back into the sitting room. "Get her upstairs to her bed, Bryce. You two have the rest of your lives together. She needs to get rested up."

The Pendletons chuckled as they left the bed and breakfast. Bryce took the key to the apartment from Mac and helped Jenny upstairs. Mac waited. He had the feeling Brenda had questions.

"Who do you think was glaring at Neb and Rachel from the window in the sitting room?" She reminded him of the incident. "Could there be a third person involved?"

"I pressed Rachel when interrogating her. She told me they made it all up. They hadn't seen anyone at all. It was on impulse. Neb came up with the idea knowing you were nearby. Neb planned to go back to the fishing hut that very night and decide what to do with Jenny but didn't count on our officers combing the property in such detail. That saved Jenny, since Neb didn't want to take the chance of being questioned about where he was going. Their ploy backfired on them. There was no third party involved in this crime at all."

"What happened to Neb and Rachel's daughter?"

"Rachel left her to grow up with her parents in Vermont while Neb was in prison. She cut ties with Neb and Rachel years ago. She is an adult now and still lives in

Vermont. She assumed Rachel's parents' last name when they legally adopted her. Neb assumed he'd be in prison for the rest of his life and allowed the adoption. Rachel didn't care about the matter and gave her consent."

"I have one last question. At least, it's one last question at the moment," Brenda said. "Has Sleazy stayed out of trouble since leaving prison?"

"He's stayed clean. I don't think he liked living behind bars all that much." Mac took her hand. "It's time for rest, Mrs. Rivers. Let's go to bed."

They met Bryce on the way down. He handed the keys to Mac and told him he and Jenny would announce their wedding plans in the next day or two. His eyes brimmed with unshed tears of happiness.

When Mac and Brenda went inside the apartment, Jenny was fast asleep. Brenda pulled the blanket up over her shoulders.

Once in bed, Mac breathed deeply. He turned to Brenda. "What a way to begin our new life together, Brenda. I didn't plan things this way."

Brenda laughed softly. "Let's face it, Mac, this is our life together. We both know what your career involves. Nothing can be predictable when it comes to crime. I understood all of that when I married you."

"I hope you don't regret it. Of course, I could look up

Natalie. Maybe you need a nanny to look after you when I leave you alone to go hunt down criminals," he teased.

"I'm sure nanny Natalie would keep me safe against the worst of the bad guys," Brenda laughed, then paused. "I would like to meet her someday, truly. She certainly did well with Jenny, who has grown into a beautiful young woman."

"Beautiful and sure of herself," Mac said. "She is so strong and came through this kidnapping ordeal like a champion." He shook his head in wonder. "It's hard to believe my little girl is now old enough to marry. That part is hard." Brenda snuggled closer to Mac, who put his strong arms around her.

The next morning, as expected, guests had dwindled. By now, everyone at Sheffield Bed and Breakfast knew the details of the criminals who had shared a space in the beautiful Queen Anne lodging with them. Brenda and Mac decided to join the guests for breakfast. Mac was prepared to answer any questions he could at this point. Both criminals were officially charged and booked until trial dates. To his surprise, only a few questions were asked.

"When did you find out Marilyn and Richard were involved?" Linda asked. "I thought she was such a nice person and would never have guessed she had a criminal background or disposition."

"Marilyn Martin was not involved at all. At this point she is not a suspect in any of it. Her husband was the one fully involved, unbeknownst to her," Mac clarified.

"That is such a relief," Linda said. "I was sure she couldn't have had anything to do with such things. I think I would have picked up on something about her if that was the case."

Conversation was muted as the guests mulled this over. Soon, most of the guests turned to talk about the Winter Festival that would begin later in the day. They were interrupted when Philip Turner came into the dining room. Several greeted him. His cheerful attitude caught everyone's attention.

"I think I got plenty of photos of the criminals. It paid off to take as many candid shots as possible. There sure is a crowd of subjects around town."

Mac made a mental note to grab the photographer before he headed for the police station. He wanted to see every photo of Neb and Rachel Tyler, and of Richard Martin, that the man had snapped.

"I'd like to see some of your work sometime before we leave," one guest said. "I'm more or less an amateur at photo shooting myself."

Philip was all too eager to show some to him. "I'll bring down what I have and anyone who wants a look is welcome. Several have been sold to two travel magazines and I hope to sell more."

Brenda wondered why Mac lingered at the table. She had a full day of preparations waiting for her attention and stood to go. She expected her husband to do the same. Instead, he waited until Philip was ready to leave and quickly followed him to the bottom of the stairs.

"I'd like to see any you have of the criminals before you take the photos down to the others."

Philip agreed and together they went to his room.

CHAPTER TEN

PHOTOS AND TOURISTS

*M*ac poured over the shots of Richard Martin in Philip's room. One photograph showed him getting into the passenger side of a grey Escape. The driver was not in sight, but since Neb Tyler owned the SUV, Mac was sure it was him. He searched through a few more. There was one more photo that clearly showed Richard and Neb standing together near the park. In the background, dusk settled in and the lights strung in the trees provided a fairyland backdrop. Mac asked Philip to send the photos he found of the two to his phone.

"I'd like to take the copies of these photos, if you don't mind. Once they are seen by Chief Ingram, then we can talk about possible reimbursement."

"As long as things are figured honestly and fairly I have

no objections," Philip said. "If there's no compensation, then I'll tell you right now there won't be a deal."

Mac didn't doubt he would receive payment, but he wanted Bob Ingram to look them over before deciding if they were worth purchasing. They went back downstairs where several guests gathered, eager to see the photographs. Philip brought a large portfolio with him. It was his chance to drum up some business.

Mac shook his head when he saw Philip wink at Allie when he passed the desk. Allie had the grace to blush.

"I'm holding you to your promise, Allie," Philip said. "I've got a front row seat reserved to get great photos of you during the competition."

"I don't think they are allowed unless you have a photographer's pass from the festival authorities."

"I have that, so I'm a step ahead of you."

When Philip went into the sitting room, Mac noticed Allie's nervousness. "Don't let him rattle you. You've practiced that routine enough to know it like the back of your hand. Forget photographers and even the audience. You'll be fine."

Allie sent a smile of relief. "I know that, but thanks, Mac. This is the first time I've competed in public like this. I don't know why Philip Turner makes me so nervous when he talks about taking photos of me."

Mac knew exactly why the young woman was so nervous and smiled gently. "Concentrate on your performance now. After you win, you can concentrate on the man who seems to be attracting your attention."

Allie blushed again. "You are right about that. He does have the ability to draw me in. I'll pay attention to your advice. Winning the competition will help pay part of my college. You know they are giving a scholarship to the winner along with the silver cup and monetary prizes."

"I know that. And that is why you are going to win."

Brenda approached and repeated Mac's encouraging words. Phyllis came in the front door as they spoke.

"It's snowing again. Everything is so beautiful. It's a perfect weekend for our Winter Festival." She removed her coat and gloves and took the wool scarf from her neck. "Now let's get busy."

Mac told them to have a good day and left them. "Before we start working, you and I must sit down and enjoy coffee together," Phyllis insisted. Both women were anxious to talk about their honeymoons, something they hadn't had time to do up to this point.

"Well, let's hide out then, or someone will find us and interrupt."

"I told you that it would be good to keep your apartment, Phyllis. Let's go."

The two drank coffee and told one another of the lovely honeymoons each had spent with their respective spouses, whose love was true and deep. Brenda was enthralled with Phyllis's descriptions of the islands she and William visited. Brenda told her she had brought back new recipes to use from Italy.

The happy honeymoon had left Phyllis in a pensive mood, reflecting on how her spouse's second marriage was a second chance at happiness. "William had a terrible marriage with Lady Pendleton, or perhaps I should simply refer to her as Priscilla. I believe they were in love at first but later discovered they had nothing in common at all." Phyllis drew a deep breath. "She wouldn't hear of divorce because she wanted everyone in Sweetfern Harbor to think theirs was a perfect marriage. Of course, as you know, Brenda, it was far from perfect. She treated him terribly."

"I know that. I still shudder when I recall finding her slumped over dead in her car right out here in front of my bed and breakfast. I was new to the area then and I think Mac somehow suspected me first of all."

"He learned his lesson, didn't he?" They laughed at the memories of Brenda's early days adjusting to Sweetfern Harbor and to Mac Rivers.

"We really need to get busy, Phyllis. I'm so glad you are home. We'll have plenty of time to chat after the festivities. I want to finish things here and get to the competition early to get a good view. I just know Allie will win."

"Of course she will. She's the best one competing."

They started in the kitchen where chef Morgan gave them several recipes to help mix up. Cookies of every flavor abounded but there still weren't enough to feed the whole town. Allie and the other employees finished decorating the downstairs where people would gather. Jenny came downstairs and demanded to help out. She looked much better and Brenda agreed she could help as long as she didn't overdo it.

By two in the afternoon, everything was ready. A break was in order. They decided to leave two employees at the bed and breakfast in case any guests hung around and needed anything. Allie was sent home to get ready for her big night. The rest of them traipsed downtown and enjoyed the many craft and food booths that lined the main street. Shops were open and crowds of people roamed around, enjoying everything on offer.

Jenny walked next to Brenda. "I want to get to my shop. I really feel well enough to work for a while. Tracy can't do all of it by herself." She noticed Brenda's worried look. "Don't worry about me. I'll take a break in back if I need one." They stopped in front of Jenny's Blossoms. "Look, someone redid my window and it looks beautiful."

"Tracy and her husband were determined to get it back

as beautiful as you created it, Jenny. You can thank them," Brenda said. They left Jenny and walked along the sidewalk. They stopped at a booth set up to cook what appeared to be full meals. The aroma of fried foods proved irresistible.

"This may be a wild request since I know you are cooking on the street, but do you have fried eggplant?" Phyllis asked.

"It's not a wild request at all," said the vendor. "We have fried eggplant patties. We'll put mozzarella cheese and tomato on top if you want it that way." Phyllis agreed happily. Brenda ordered a fried haddock sandwich and sweet potato fries.

They took their orders to one of the tables set up at the edge of the piles of snow that had been pushed to the curb. Hot beverages steamed before them. They ate and then browsed some of the other booths. Finally, they made their way to Morning Sun Coffee, where they finished with hot chocolate.

"I can't believe you two ate sitting out in that cold weather," Molly said. "You could have brought it in here with you and sat where it's warm."

The two women laughed. "We didn't mind. It felt good to sit out there and pretend it was summer. Lots of people did the same thing." Brenda added that the hot food warmed them.

Brenda said she wanted to relieve the two employees at the bed and breakfast so they could enjoy the activity downtown. They were a block from Sheffield Bed and Breakfast when Brenda recognized a familiar voice. She turned to see Marilyn Martin talking with two women and three men. They all appeared friendly and Brenda presumed they knew one another.

Marilyn noticed Brenda and waved to her. "It's a wonderful festival," she said. Her former guest didn't bother introducing Brenda to her friends and chattered on about activities around them until Brenda excused herself, stating she needed to get back to her business.

"That seemed strange," Brenda commented once out of earshot. When Phyllis questioned her, Brenda told her she had no idea Marilyn Martin knew anyone around town.

"Maybe she just met them today or at the motel where she's staying. You told me she befriended one of your guests right away when she got here."

Brenda had to agree that Marilyn seemed to make friends easily and dismissed her misgivings. At least she was sticking around Sweetfern Harbor until Mac finished with any questioning of her. Once back at the bed and breakfast, Phyllis filled the two employees in on what was going on downtown. She sat with Brenda in the sitting room to wait. The door was open so they would know when anyone came in. Guests began to trickle in after an hour or so. Brenda invited them in for a hot beverage and refreshments. Several took her up on the invitation and joined them.

"I thought Marilyn left town," Linda said, "but I just saw her down near the shops."

"She moved to different lodgings because she felt more comfortable doing so. Phyllis and I spoke with her. She is staying in town until the Winter Festival is over." The explanation satisfied Linda and the guests talked of the delicious food cooked on the street. Brenda told them that Allie would compete later in the ice skating competition. "They will skate on the frozen lake at the park. Make sure you dress warmly. It will last a couple of hours by the time everything is finished."

"There will be a break after the first hour so you can go to the warming stations they'll have set up," Phyllis said.

"If anyone needs warm coats or gloves or even boots, let me know. We keep a stash here for guests." Two ladies mentioned they would probably add to their wardrobe for the night.

It was finally time for the competition to begin. The crowd that gathered sat on makeshift bleachers at the edge of the frozen lake and huddled together. Winds were calm and it was a starry night.

Allie waited with Hope by her side, behind the partition that circled the smooth ice that was illuminated with spotlights in the darkness. Her mother's presence calmed her considerably and Allie knew she was ready as soon as her name was called. *Imagine* began and she glided onto the slate-like ice. Her movements were perfection. Allie's eyes roved over the crowd but she didn't focus on any one person, not even Philip Turner, whose camera was taking bursts of shots every time she gracefully swooped or turned over the frozen surface.

"She's mouthing the words," Brenda said. "See, I just saw her mouth the words 'you say I'm a dreamer.' She's really into it." Mac nodded and on her left Phyllis whispered agreement.

David Williams leaned over her shoulder from behind them. "*Imagine* is her favorite and she is crazy about John Lennon's songs. She told me she sings along as she skates because she can really get into her movements." He paused and watched his daughter. "She's something, isn't she?"

Brenda turned around. "Yes, she sure is and she's a winner tonight. I'm sure of it."

Brenda was right. At the end when the winners were announced, Allie Williams came in first. Everyone clapped and shouted congratulations her way. Allie beamed brighter than the sparkling lights that shimmered across the frozen lake. When everyone arrived at Sheffield Bed and Breakfast, no one talked of anything other than how beautiful Allie was on the ice. They marveled at her ability to perform so flawlessly. Brenda told her again and again how talented she was.

Allie whispered to Brenda. "I hope to be a professional skater someday and maybe make it to the Olympics."

"I don't doubt you will succeed, Allie."

The tourists, guests and townspeople in Sweetfern Harbor came and went through Sheffield Bed and Breakfast. They enjoyed the sweets the chef had prepared and many compliments were thrown out about the large pretzels supplied by Sweet Treats. Mac reached for a second bacon cheddar pretzel and picked up a small container of queso dip. Brenda suggested he try one of the cinnamon sugar ones, too.

"I may regret having this second bacon and cheddar. It's hard to choose from all these goodies. You did a wonderful job as usual," he told her.

Bryce and Jenny joined them. She held half a pretzel in one hand and ranch dip in the other. "I would learn to make these but it's a surer thing if I just buy them in the future from Hope." She explained hers was honey and garlic. "Not too much garlic, but just the hint of it is delicious."

They joked about Bryce staying away from her if she insisted on eating garlic. Brenda smiled to see that her loved ones were so relaxed. The happy babble of voices around her told her that everyone was enjoying feelings of security around town once again.

"I'm going to catch up with some of the shopkeepers I haven't seen since coming home from Italy," Brenda said.

She turned away and then stopped when she heard Mac's phone ring. She glanced back to see regret in his eyes. He handed her his half-eaten pretzel and pulled her aside.

"There's trouble down at the jail. I have to get moving." He grabbed Bryce and told him they were on their way to the police station. "Seems someone tried to free our two notorious prisoners while we were all celebrating."

"Are you telling me they are loose on the streets?" Brenda asked.

"No," Mac said, "but the would-be jail breakers are. Let's go, Bryce."

Brenda and Jenny looked at one another. Then Brenda started toward the front door of her bed and breakfast. She wanted to know who came and went from this point forward.

"Phyllis and I will go to the back door," Jenny said, as she signaled Phyllis.

Brenda recognized two plainclothes police officers already in the foyer. Phyllis and Jenny found the same security at the back and side doors. Brenda meandered through the crowd of people in her establishment. Most were familiar to her, but with so many tourists in town it was impossible to know who everyone was. Her stomach dropped to realize she had no idea if they were friend or foe.

Allie found Brenda after hearing murmurs from several guests who had been near Brenda and Mac when the detectives suddenly left the party. She and Brenda met in a quiet spot in the hallway. Allie asked what was going on.

"There has been an attempted jail break. At least, I hope it was only an attempt. Mac and Bryce are down there investigating. Let's try to keep things going as if nothing unusual is happening. Keep your eyes open. We don't know who tried to break them out. I just hope no more guests were involved."

Allie gasped. "You're right. They could be hiding in plain sight." Brenda reminded her to stay calm. When the young reservationist walked away from Brenda, something struck her as odd. She called Allie back.

"Where is your admirer, the photographer?"

"I haven't seen Philip since he tried to distract me during the competition. His ego may have been damaged when I didn't take the bait."

Brenda agreed with Allie. Once she walked back into the crowd, Brenda searched for her guest. Philip Turner was absent. Phyllis caught up with Brenda and Brenda asked her if she had seen the photographer.

"I haven't seen him since the competition. That's a little surprising since you'd think he would want to keep snapping pictures all the way to the end of the celebrations," said Phyllis.

The women looked at one another. Brenda saw one of the plainclothes cops and asked him to come upstairs to the photographer's room with her. She lowered her voice and warned him she had no idea what, if anything, they would find. Officer Patrick Simpson followed them too when he asked Brenda what was going on. Together, the two cops and Brenda went to Philip's room. She knocked on the door and, receiving no answer, unlocked it.

The room was empty. The only indication anyone had occupied the room was the rumpled bed covers. The armoire was empty and no suitcases were in sight. Brenda told Patrick to search for anything that may give a hint as to who the photographer really was while she called Mac. She told her husband about the missing man.

"Finally, we have someone to look for," Mac said. "So far, neither prisoner will tell us anything."

CHAPTER ELEVEN

NOT SO INNOCENT

The rest of the evening went smoothly at Sheffield Bed and Breakfast. When the last guest left, only the female and male police officers in plainclothes remained. They were ordered by Mac to stay where they were and keep their eyes open for Philip Turner. Brenda thanked her employees for a successful night and everyone left except chef Morgan and her helpers, who finished putting things away in the kitchen. Brenda thanked them and was glad only she, Jenny and Phyllis were left with the officers. The three women sat in the sitting room. Brenda waited until Officer Simpson returned to give her any news of findings in Philip's room.

"We found some scraps of paper, blank ones, and this was sticking out from under the bed. It looks like your guest left a very important document by mistake." He shook his head. "I don't know how anyone would so carelessly leave a passport on the floor."

"He probably dropped it without knowing it." Brenda read the name on the passport. It showed the correct name, and country of origin was Canada. That was crucial to prove at least one person in the drama was who he said he was. She called Mac to give him the update. "He can't get out of the United States without his passport, at least."

Brenda felt the smile in Mac's voice. "No, he cannot."

Philip Turner was sure he could successfully free Neb and Richard. It would be easy. Everyone, including the cops, would be at the big celebration at the bed and breakfast. He knew the local sheriff and one deputy were at the police station guarding the jail cells, and no one else. When he slipped through the back door, he heard them laughing in a room down the hall. It sounded as if they were playing cards. The men he intended to free were at the opposite end. Philip didn't expect such good luck. He crept down the hall and when he got to the first cell where Neb was held, he held his finger to his lips. Neb grinned.

Things were going well. Philip watched his father for many years unlock every type of lock when people forgot or lost keys to their cars or homes. Philip himself became a locksmith as a young adult. His side hobby was always photography, and he found that posing as a photographer was an easy disguise that also helped win him points with pretty girls on occasion.

When Neb and Richard were accused of their crimes, he had used his festival press pass to get in the jail to snap photos. He noted the poorly maintained cell door locks and managed to get two photos detailing the lock pieces. He had laughed to himself at the failure of those in charge to see that there was a gap between the door frame and the slam lock on three cells in a row. Neb and Richard were each assigned one of them. It was sheer luck that the police officer hadn't come across any of the photos of the jail cells when he had reviewed the photos in his hotel room the other day.

At Neb's cell, Philip moved the pry bar from his left hand to his right and began prying. He panicked when he clanged the bar against the door frame, freezing in place. The laughing and sounds of camaraderie from down the hall stopped.

Neb knew Philip was his only hope on the outside, but the overconfident young man had blown his chance. "Get out, you idiot," he hissed. "We'll think of something else. Run."

Philip held onto the pry bar tightly and escaped the police station the way he had come in, his dark form melting into the darkness of the rear parking lot. The sheriff sent his deputy out the back door while he quickly ascertained the cell doors were still locked. Then he went after them. The deputy turned to him and spread his hands in frustration.

"I lost him." He pointed to the dark alley.

The sheriff called Detective Mac Rivers right away. Neither officer had a good look at the would-be jail breaker except to say he had light-colored hair and was rather tall. A manhunt began.

Philip Turner had already packed his bags securely in the trunk of his car. He calculated how long it would take him to get to the Canadian border and turned the ignition. He wanted to speed to get there faster but he realized he couldn't risk being stopped for a traffic violation. Once across the border and safely home it would be a long process to find him and prove he was the one who tried to free his cousin Neb Tyler and Neb's co-conspirator Richard. He and Neb had grown up together like brothers. Neb was two years older than Philip and that alone caused the man to lord it over his younger cousin. Philip was a follower and Neb was afraid of nothing.

When Neb told him he and Rachel were going to spend a long weekend in the remote town of Sweetfern Harbor, he asked him why he would want to go somewhere with no action.

"There will be plenty of action, Phil," Neb told him. "Come with us. You might get some good pictures around that town." He went on to tell Philip of the upcoming celebrations.

Philip pressed him to tell him the real reason. His cousin had only recently gotten out of prison and he didn't trust him to stay out of trouble. Philip was swayed as usual by his cousin, but when Philip asked the real reason, Neb hesitated. Philip had never been in trouble with the law before. He was incredulous when Neb finally revealed that he planned to get revenge on a top cop.

He hated himself when he caved in. "I don't want any part of crime," he told Neb. "If you want me to take pictures of people to help your cause then I'll go that far but I won't do anything else to help you."

Neb's laugh was not reassuring. "I don't expect to get caught, but if I do, I want you to promise me you will come to the station and get some vital pictures of my arrest."

Philip had shivered. "What do you mean by vital pictures?"

"Pictures of the locks on the cell doors, of course. If I'm put behind bars again, I'll count on you getting me out. I'm really lucky, Phil, to have a cousin who is a good locksmith and loyal friend to the end."

When Philip didn't respond, Neb egged him on like they

were children again. Philip agreed he would take pictures of the detective and anyone else that seemed important around Sweetfern Harbor, but he drew the line at getting him out of jail if it came to that. When push came to shove though, once again Philip did what his cousin told him to do.

And now he was on the run. If he made it across the border, he'd have nothing to worry about. Neb was still behind locked bars and he couldn't drag Philip further into this mess. The photographer didn't worry about Neb telling the cops he was the one who tried to break him out. He was sure he would be long escaped to his home country by then. He wasn't so sure about Neb's friend Richard, but what proof did he have? He eyed the speedometer and carefully pressed the gas pedal down to the fastest but safest speed he was willing to drive.

Brenda and Phyllis paced until William finally told them to sit down or do something other than wear out the hardwood floor.

"I'm going to the police station," Brenda said. "I want to talk to Richard Martin again. He will talk easier than Neb Tyler ever will."

All three put their winter coats on. William and Phyllis followed Brenda. When they got to the police station,

Brenda headed for Chief Ingram's office. He looked up in surprise.

"It's after midnight, Brenda. What are you doing down here?"

"It seems I'm responsible for housing yet another criminal at my bed and breakfast. Maybe I can help. Did Neb or Richard admit it was Philip Turner who tried to get them out?"

"They aren't talking, but from what you told us you found, we are sure it is the photographer."

"He has to be more than a photographer. In fact, from the way things have unfolded so far, I feel very sure that is just a ruse. If he knows how to break locks, he could be a locksmith. I want to talk to Richard Martin."

Chief Ingram didn't hesitate. "Fine with me, Brenda. We've moved them back into the interrogation rooms, keeping them both awake, hoping they'll confirm it was Turner." He signaled one of the officers to allow Brenda access to Richard in one of the interrogation rooms.

She sat across from him and finally looked him in the eye. "It seems I've allowed more than a few criminals to sully my fine bed and breakfast. You owe me something, Richard." He couldn't look at her. Instead, he bowed his head. Moisture prickled across his forehead. "You owe me a lot, actually. Who tried to get the two of you out of jail while we all celebrated? It had to be someone familiar with the cell locks. Was it another cop?"

Richard looked hopeful at first but something in her eyes told him she knew it hadn't been a cop. He tried to wring his hands but the handcuffs prevented that. "It wasn't a cop. It was a friend of Neb's. I don't know his name."

"I'm sure you know his name and can describe him perfectly."

By now perspiration began to trickle. "It was that photographer that stayed at the bed and breakfast. He's a photographer but he's also a locksmith."

Brenda prodded until Richard finally explained that Philip Turner and Neb Tyler were cousins. "I don't think he's ever been in trouble with the law before like Neb. I think Neb has a hold on him somehow and made him agree."

Brenda left him to stew in his deeds and knowledge. She told Chief Ingram the news. Mac and Bryce were on the hunt along with other law enforcement.

A few minutes later the phone rang. "Good, good work, everyone," the chief said. He looked at Brenda. "Turner hadn't made it to the border when they caught him. Of course, he couldn't have crossed anyway since he didn't have his passport, plus Border Patrol was notified to stop him if he tried."

By the time Mac and Bryce returned to the police station, Brenda and Bob were chatting about the success of the Winter Festival as if the turmoil had not ensued at all. William and Phyllis had gone home several hours ago. Mac's face lit up when he saw Brenda. He kissed her and hugged her tightly.

"Thanks for your hard work in this," he told her. "Let's go home and get a good sleep. Tomorrow we will take a day trip up the coast and enjoy our winter wonderland."

"Nothing would please me more than to have a peaceful day just with you, Mac. It's hard to imagine what that will be like."

"I don't have to imagine, Brenda. I already know what a lucky man I am to have you."

Chief Ingram waved them away with a smile. Mac took Brenda's hand and together they walked out into the starry, crisp night air.

ABOUT THE AUTHOR

Wendy Meadows is an emerging author of cozy mysteries. She lives in "The Granite State" with her husband, two sons, two cats and lovable Labradoodle.

When she isn't working on her stories she likes to tend to her flowers, relax with her pets and play video games with her family.

Get in Touch with Wendy
www.wendymeadows.com

amazon.com/author/wendymeadows

goodreads.com/wendymeadows

bookbub.com/authors/wendy-meadows

facebook.com/AuthorWendyMeadows

twitter.com/wmeadowscozy